P9-DYJ-359

Capote in Kansas

A Ghost Story

Kim Powers

CARROLL & GRAF PUBLISHERS
NEW YORK

For Jess, as always . . .
And in loving memory of Frieda Badian Goldstein

CAPOTE IN KANSAS
A Ghost Story

Copyright © 2007 by Kim Powers

First Carroll & Graf edition 2007

This is a work of fiction, suggested by certain incidents
in the lives of its two main characters.

All rights reserved. No part of this book may be reproduced in whole
or in part without written permission from the publisher, except by
reviewers who may quote brief excerpts in connection with a review in
a newspaper, magazine, or electronic publication; nor may any part of
this book be reproduced, stored in a retrieval system, or transmitted
in any form or by any means electronic, mechanical, photocopying,
recording, or other, without written permission from the publisher.

Library of Congress Cataloging-in-Publication Data is available.

ISBN-10: 0-7867-2033-6
ISBN-13: 978-0-7867-2033-0

9 8 7 6 5 4 3 2 1

Printed in the United States of America
Interior Design by Bettina Whilhelm

Chapter One

"She's back. She's after me."

Those were the first words Nelle had heard from him in—God, twenty years? However many years it had been, it was so long ago she couldn't remember. She just knew that it had been another time, another place.

She also knew immediately, even with the call coming in the middle of the night, who it was. Even a deaf and nearly dead old person—which she wasn't, but getting there—could tell who was on the other end of the line, the high-pitched, nasal whine as unmistakable at age fifty-nine as it had been fifty years earlier.

"Truman?"

"I'm in trouble. Terrible, terrible, terrible trouble."

"Truman. Good Lord Above, I can't believe . . ."

"Trouble like you won't believe. Oh, Nelle, Nellynellynelly, I've messed up, you've gotta help me."

"I believe *all* the trouble I hear about you, but let's start with how dare you call me outta the blue when you haven't called in . . ."

He cut her off, unrepentant, nothing like a little "I'm sorry we haven't talked in twenty years" to stand in his way.

He was in trouble and he needed help *now*.

"You're the only one I can trust. I've written a book, my masterpiece, all my secrets, all *their* secrets, and now she's trying to steal it, take it from me 'fore it's ready . . ."

"Who? Where *are* you?"

"In Palm Springs. In Cold Blood," he added, a giggle, a postscript. "Oh, Nelle . . ."

Now he was crying.

"First it was all those bitches in New York, the ones I wrote about, who practically drummed me out of town. Now it's her. I can't get her to leave. I don't *want* her here."

"*Who* are you talkin' about?"

"Nancy. I told you."

No, he hadn't, and Nancy who? She didn't know any Nancy.

"She's come here every night in a row now, and I'm scared."

"*Who* has been comin'?"

An exasperated sigh. "*Nancy. Nancy Clutter. Remember?*"

"You idiot," he might as well have said.

Nancy Clutter.

From In *Cold Blood*.

The dead teenage girl who loved horses.

Jesus H. Christ.

His coming couldn't have been any more surprising.

"She's here. In this very room, over in the corner. Just staring at me. And I'm scared witless. Shitless," he said, giggled again, then cried. Again. "She's just staring at me—ohsweetJesusLord—now she's at the foot of the bed. How'dshegethereshit."

"Throw a bottle at her. Sounds like you've got a few lyin' around."

Nelle was not having any of this, no matter how drunk or scared or famous he was. Not a word of explanation for disappearing on her—blaspheming her—years ago. She was not a retiring woman, about to roll over and accept table scraps. Just read her book—she had one too, you know—and find out. She'd been a tomboy, tough as nails, able to punch out anybody on the playground, and she still had it in her. It was old, and tired, and arthritic, but it was still there. Tough. It took being tough to deal with all the requests and questions and letters that came her way.

But this—from a man half her size, half her strength, a voice way higher than hers, one call—and she caved.

"Now she's jabbering . . ."

"What? What's she saying?"

Like the dead Nancy Clutter was actually talking to Truman. Nelle could not believe herself. What indeed.

"She's blaming me. And you, too . . ."

"Me?"

". . . You were there, too, Miss Don't Think You're Gonna Get Outta This So Easy."

"Blamin' us? For what?" (Indignant at a ghost that wasn't there. Nelle was losing her mind, same as Truman.)

Finally, a pause on the other end, as if Truman couldn't quite believe what Nancy had just said, and was trying to process her words before he repeated them to Nelle.

"Blaming us because . . . I made her famous. *We* made her famous. She says she never wanted to be famous. Would *you* wanna be famous for getting killed?"

Famous.

Mad at being famous—the only thing Truman had ever wanted to be.

The only thing Nelle had never wanted to be.

That shut all three of them up.

For a second.

"What the fuck do I do now?" he hissed, more angry than scared at the ghost of the young girl whose murder had made him a household name and destroyed his life.

"Truman, it's the middle of the night. Go to sleep, call me tomorrow . . ."

"Go to sleep? I might not *be* here tomorrow! I'm about to get murdered in my sleep and you're worried about missing out on some *dreams*, which, if they're anything like mine, are terrifying enough to begin with without some specter intruding . . ."

There was a pause; Truman was shifting around, moving the receiver.

"Here, you talk to her. You'll know what to say. You always did. You're the one who sweet-talked those Kansas hicks in the first place. She's just another Kansas hick, even if she's dead. Do it again."

For one second, Nelle thought: how insensitive could he be, calling Nancy Clutter a Kansas hick to her face—her dead face—then she remembered you couldn't offend someone WHO WASN'T THERE.

Nelle heard the receiver on the other end get shuffled around; Truman was holding it out to Nancy.

Nancy Clutter, back for him.

He deserved it.

They both deserved it.

Then, another voice; it was muffled, but it was there, and Nelle almost dropped the phone.

It WAS Nancy Clutter, speaking from the grave.

No—how STUPID could Nelle be—it was just Truman's maid; a black woman's voice, Nelle heard that clearly enough. You didn't grow up in the South without being able to hear that.

"This Myrtle Bennett, Mr. Truman's girl?"

"Girl my ass," Nelle heard Truman snort in the background; he wasn't too drunk or terrified for sarcasm. "You're old! And you're fat! Just like me! Now GO AWAY!" That was Truman, yelling not at his maid, but at Nancy, followed by the sound of a bottle crashing into a wall.

"He's sick, awful sick, drinkin' to beat the band . . ."

"I have just had a few drinks, no more than normal, and you would, too, if a *ghost* . . ."

". . . and you're all he's been talkin' 'bout for hours so I dug through his things and found your number and . . ."

The phone went dead, just like Nancy Clutter.

Nelle wasn't going back to sleep now; there were ghosts everywhere she turned.

And they were coming for her, as well.

———

She'd been having her own night visitors lately, and not just Truman, with his tales of Nancy Clutter. For a Southern girl, with the swampy, hazy bayou at her feet, it was strange that she hadn't believed in ghosts before now, but she hadn't. She'd gone to law school, for God's sake. Ghosts played no part in the practice of the law. It was only as she became older—hell, got old—that she had come to believe so fervently in them. They haunted her sleep now, what little sleep came: ghosts of her mother and father and brother Ed—who had died so suddenly and unexpectedly, the one she missed most of all, even after all these years. People kept asking if she still wrote; that's almost all they ever asked. It would amaze them to know she'd been writing every day and night for the past forty years—one long, unbroken letter to her brother Ed, every single day.

Ghosts.

A call in the middle of the night.

This isn't how she wanted it to be.

Her first words from Truman in years—this "pocket-sized Merlin," as she'd anointed him in The Book—and he was drunk and hallucinating. No apology, no catching up, no explanation, just "Save me" . . .

No.

She was old, and couldn't move that fast anymore. She wanted, she needed, time to reflect, time to drift into a reverie about their shared childhoods, about barefoot summers and feet so calloused by the hot earth nothing could hurt them, about lemonade and cake and talcum powder smells and starched white linen, which he always wore, even on the hottest days, but . . .

No.

She was too old for this, an unwelcome voice from the past.

Anybody's voice, dead or alive, or just dead to her.

A flat dial tone came from the phone she still gripped in her hand. An old person's hand, she thought, drifting into writer's mode: blood veins ridged like highways that dropped off on both sides, liver spots melding into a tan, turkey skin that wouldn't fall back into place after you pinched it up.

She replaced the receiver on its cradle—no clue how to get Truman back, no clue if she *wanted* to get Truman back—and sat up straighter in bed, her face rising into view in her bureau mirror, against the wall.

She was in her late fifties, but looked older because of all the time she spent out in the Alabama sun: wrinkled, leathery skin as dry as those hot summers when she'd first met Truman. No amount of fancy moisturizer or suntan lotion her sister Alice tried to force on her would change all that, a trophy from Nelle's days on her beloved golf course.

Nelle often saw Truman's photograph, and knew the years had been as unkind to him, even with all his reported nips and tucks: his skin was just as leathery and parched and thirsty as hers, no amount of surgery could make up for that. A sad homecoming for someone who had been the most beautiful, flawless child she'd ever seen. Strange, she knew, a child, especially a tomboy like her, knowing another child was beautiful, but she did. Everyone knew that about Truman, who had the most perfect skin anyone had ever seen, an ageless alien in their midst. But then you moved past his perfect skin and cellophane-clear hair to his eyes, and saw that all the worry and age had gone into them. They were ancient, primordial. He was an old soul, always had been; it was clear he knew things, had seen things, even at seven years old.

He had lived next door to her, at least for three months out of the year, for most of her childhood. Every summer when he came to Monroeville—deposited with relatives there by his socialite mother, who lived in New York and had Better Things to Do, and no time or use for her lone (and lonely) child—they would fall back into their familiar pattern of cub reporter and recording secretary; he had the words, she had the typing skill (learned on the old Underwood typewriter her father kept at home). And, as befitting the tomboy daughter of a lawyer father, and a little boy whose most loyal companion was his imagination, their favorite stories were crimes, the gorier the better. Truman, puffing out his lower lip and blowing upward to get his spiderweb-fine hair out of his eyes, would write them down in a little notebook he always carried; Nelle would do the legwork.

When they didn't have a real mystery to solve—which was most of the time, even though everything was a mystery to a lonely and sensitive southern child—they'd make one up, each adding gruesome twist after twist to the plot, the better to out-spook the other. One particular summer's story had repulsed, and thus fascinated, them, even more: a man's body, puffed up and bloated, had been found in the river, the unfortunate victim of a cottonmouth snake. They decided the bloating was in equal parts from being waterlogged and from the snake's deadly toxin. They couldn't decide which was worse—or, in their lexicon, better.

What ghoulish children they had been, salivating over the details of how some poor soul had met his Maker.

And now, they had come full circle: Nancy Clutter—who had met her Maker in a spectacularly horrible and public way—was back for them.

—

She wasn't alone.

Truman called Nelle the next night as well.

This time, the ghost belonged to Kenyon, Nancy's fifteen-year-old brother. At first, Nelle wanted to laugh: so that's how Truman was going to play this, have the whole Clutter family haunt him, one by one; but he was so terrified she knew it was real, if only to him.

Kenyon, as described by an hysterical Truman, was different from Nancy. He didn't say a word—no blame for fame, at least—just silently threatened Truman with the glowing tip of a cigarette, no doubt an invitation to remember the scene Truman had invented in which Kenyon's father, Herb, caught him smoking in the basement, the basement where they would spend the last few moments of their lives. (Truman invented a lot of scenes; not many people knew that. Maybe that's why Kenyon was so smoldering.)

When Truman called a third night in a row, Nelle wasn't surprised. She'd been expecting, even looking forward to, the voice that sounded more southern with each successive call, forcing herself to stay awake even though her pills had begun to kick in and draw her to sleep. By now, Truman's ghosts were becoming hers as well; she was afraid of sleep for almost the first time in her life, afraid those same phantoms might be on the other side of her closed eyelids. She had been with Truman in Kansas, after all, had seen and heard the same things he had. Why should she be exempt from a ghost or two?

She was only surprised at who Truman's phantom was this time.

"Perry," he said.

That was a switch.

Perry Smith.

No longer one of the Clutters, part of the family, but one of their killers.

Truman sounded even more drunk than he had the first two nights.

"Son 'bitch is right here, rubbing his crotch in my face. Says I should'a saved him, got my big city friends to save him, but I didn't, and now I'm going down just like him . . . he's calling me a 'little faggot.'"

Now Truman was crying.

Nelle had heard it all before. She had heard it—and said it—during the endless, agonizing years when Truman was trying to finish his masterwork, delayed by the unfortunate slowness of reality, and the legal system, when appeal after appeal kept the killers from the gallows, and he didn't have an ending. She'd nursed Truman with her words then; she would nurse him with the same words now.

"Nothing could have saved him, Truman. You know it and I know it and he knows it." ("He does NOT know it, because he's not THERE," she thought to herself, even in the midst of talking to Truman.) "He confessed."

The tears were flowing.

"I'm dreaming of the Clutters' house—WHEN THEY FUCKIN' LEAVE ME ALONE, THAT IS, AND I CAN ACTUALLY SLEEP FOR TWO GODDAMN SECONDS—and of poor little Nancy and Kenyon, Perry killing them, their parents, too, all for money he thought was in the house but wasn't, and I just get sick, physically sick, I wake up covered with vomit, the thought of him putting the pillow under Nancy's little head, making her more comfortable for . . . makes me wanna puke." ("AND I DO," he yells at the ghost.) "I wanna give him all my money and say, 'Here, Perry, take it, just leave them alone. Leave ME alone.'"

Nelle barely knew what to say, even in the dark of night, when truth was easiest. But she didn't have to say anything, because Truman rambled on, trying to come up with a too-late remedy for his own salvation or, at the very least, sleep.

"And I would, too. Give him every last penny of mine. Every last penny of ill-gotten gain . . ."

Perry was Truman's, not hers, and always had been; trying to get between the two of them would be like trying to come between two lovers. Even worse: two lovers who knew they shouldn't be together, but couldn't break apart. Truman had tried to argue that Perry was a victim himself, in his own right—of a miserable childhood. "*Victim?*" Nelle had argued right back, having predicted that Truman would fall in love with Perry the moment he laid eyes on him. "He's a killer. *In Cold Blood*. It's your title, can't say it any plainer than that. Victim my ass." There was nothing Nelle could say or do about Perry and there never had been, so she let Truman ramble on, as her gaze went once again to her face in the mirror.

Instead of the craggy old thing she usually saw there—looking back at her as if asking, "What do YOU want?"—she saw the bright, hopeful young woman she had been in her twenties, when she had been alert and eager to please. It had been a forthright, friendly face, hadn't it, one people liked, before she'd taught herself to be so Goddamn scary? Before she'd turned herself, intentionally or not, into Boo Radley, her Frankenstein, made up of bits and pieces? What were the bits and pieces that had made her up, and brought her to this place where people were afraid of her—but she was even more afraid of them? That was Boo's secret of secrets: he was even more afraid of them.

Nelle saw, as her mind traveled back, her young face looking into Truman's even younger face; if she looked to be in her early thirties, which she was when their true haunting began, he looked to be about twelve.

Twelve with a bad French accent.

It was almost twenty-five years ago.

—

"I'd like to purchase two round-trip tickets to Kansas, s'il vous plait."

France, by way of the deep South.

Truman's delicate little hands—Nelle could swear he'd had a manicure, his fingernails were so shiny and pink—plunked down two wads of money on the counter of the airline reservations desk where she worked in New York.

"Truman, what are you doing here?" And then, under her breath, "I'm busy. I'm working." Her emphasis on the word made it clear it was something he should be doing, as well, but as he was already the published author of several novels and short stories, she didn't really know what his work now entailed.

"I AM working, for your information, just like everyone else here . . . even though I'm NOT like everyone else. Here or elsewhere."

With a scarf wrapped around his neck and trailing, Isadora Duncan–like, at least three feet behind him—fluttering magically when there was no breeze, as if he had his own wind machine—that was abundantly clear: he WASN'T like anyone else.

"I'll see you after I get off. At five."

"I'm serious. I'm here for the purpose of commerce. I want to buy two tickets to Kansas."

"It's flat. You won't like it. I've seen the brochures."

"Two tickets. One for me, one for you. We're going there, to look into the heart of darkness."

That got her attention, in a way his bizarreness couldn't. She'd known him since childhood. She was used to his bizarreness.

"A murder . . . a murder has been perpetrated, four members of the same family gunned down, knifed, in cold blood. Mr. William Shawn of the esteemed *New Yorker* magazine is sending me there to write about it. That, or follow a housecleaner around Manhattan, and write about the people she works for, based on what's in their apartments. I decided a bunch of rich people in this town is far scarier than anyone in Kansas, killers on the loose or not. And you're going to help."

"Excuse me?"

"I need an assistant."

"An assistant."

"A consort," he amended, afraid his choice of words would anger her and queer the deal, because the whole plan was contingent on her going. He conveniently forgot to tell her that someone else had already passed on the assignment; that she was, literally, sloppy seconds. He reached over the counter and picked some remnant from her lunch break off her collar. The task at hand was scary enough—a murderer on the loose on the fruited plains—but it would be impossible without Nelle by his side, greasing the wheels, using her particular small-town charm to get people to open up to him, and, when push came to shove, using her sheer size to scare the interviews out of the good folks of Holcomb, Kansas.

"I've got a job, in case you haven't noticed; it might not be the one of my dreams, but for now . . ."

"A ridiculous job, in an equally ridiculous uniform."

"I'll tell the president of the company you think so, next time he's in town."

She hated to admit Truman was right: it was a ridiculous job, a ridiculous uniform, and she hated it. But since her long-in-the-works book might never amount to anything, it was a ridiculous job she needed.

Truman continued. "It'll take your mind off things, while you're waiting for your bird book to come out. And it'll be like old times, us solving a mystery together. Besides, I think we're still engaged. We should put in an appearance together, just for propriety's sake. People are beginning to talk."

Their engagement, enacted when she was six and he was an older man of seven years old—*will you marry me? yeah, I guess*, a quick peck on the cheek, forgotten until he returned to town the next summer—was the stuff of local legend, back in the town from which they had both escaped.

"I've already written your letter, asking for a leave of absence. I'll even autograph it, if you like. We leave in three days."

"Three days," Nelle said, appalled but intrigued. Truman's siren song of murder was deep calling to deep. She wanted to quit right there on the spot, but she couldn't let him win.

Truman always won.

As he sashayed out of the building, his victory all but assured, he added over his shoulder, "And of course, you'll need to buy a gun. As much to protect us against the good people of Kansas as the real killers."

"If you're 'fraid enough to need a gun, then why go?"

He had to, he said; the Clutters were calling him, he could hear them already.

Three days later, Nelle was on her way to Kansas with him, gun slyly, dutifully purchased and packed in the bottom of a suitcase. They were on a train instead of a plane, even though she could have gotten them her employee discount.

—

"Get the fuck away."

"What?" The words made Nelle furrow her eyes in the mirror, as she saw she wasn't a girl of thirty anymore, but an old woman, talking to a man who had abandoned her long ago.

Truman was still going on about Perry.

"He won't go. He's got a noose burn around his neck, and an erection. I can see it through the fabric of his pants. It happens when they're hung." He laughed at his own joke, then started choking. "Why am I joking? They're expecting a book, but it's not done. What am I gonna do?"

Nelle was about to say "Quit drinking" in her no-nonsense way, but out of the blue—as out of the blue as Truman's call had been— he had switched subjects, to the thing he was really afraid of.

The real reason for these calls late at night, when the cover of darkness could camouflage the truth.

It was the truth of a little boy who was all alone, who knew he was different, who knew his mother hadn't loved him, no matter how hard he tried to not let on to anybody else.

Who knew he couldn't write anymore.

"I try, I try so hard, I wake up and my hands hurt so much from all the writing I do . . . these beautiful hands, there's a blood blister the size of one of your golf balls on the finger where my pen scrapes against it all day long and comes up with nothing . . ."

A call, a call for help, late at night, when the world was at rest and he was too drunk to tell anything but the truth: "I've burned page after page. They're just no good. The burning's the only thing that has any juice left in it."

There, in the middle of the night, her sister asleep in the next room, Nelle revealed her truth, as well: "Me, too."

"I can't write anymore, Nelly. There's no drama left. Just the drama of my life. But I can't get that down on the page anymore."

That was the scariest thing in Truman's life—not Nancy Clutter or Kenyon Clutter or Perry Smith, who had killed four people in cold blood.

This was a whole other kind of ghost story.

"You've gotta help me. Be my . . . consort, just like in Kansas. Don't let them take my book. Don't let them find me out." A pause, then, "Remember Kansas?"

"Of course I do. What else have we been talkin' about?"

"I need that, I need the past right now, just hold me over the phone and tell me a bedtime story about Kansas . . . tell me about the past, Nelle, tell me about the last good time. Tell me about our childhood, when we weren't scary or scared and we'd hide in the graveyard . . ."

And then the phone slipped from his fingers.

After a pause—"Truman? Tru? You still there? Don't go, it's okay, give me your number"—someone gently hung up the receiver on his end.

Whether it was Myrtle, Truman's maid, or Perry Smith, back from the dead, or one of the Clutter children, Nelle couldn't even begin to guess.

Chapter Two

Truman was in love with the air-conditioner man.

Myrtle didn't approve, but there was nothing she could do about it. If he wanted to run around on Mr. Jack, his friend back in New York, that was his business, not hers. Her only business was that it was Palm Springs, it was hot, and the AC never worked worth a tinker's damn. Leave it to a white man like Truman to go and pay all that money for a fancy little cracker box of a house, complete with a swimming pool, then go and have the AC break down every time you looked at it. And with the sun blazing through the one wall that was all plate glass window, there was nothing to do but practically make the air conditioner man part of the family—even if he already had one of his own, with a wife and two sons.

The AC man came once, he came twice, and soon, he was coming all the time. Truman roared when Myrtle said that; she didn't know why. When she asked, in all innocence, what kind of "power tools" he had at his disposal, Truman snorted so hard his orange drink came spurting out of his nose.

Danny. She might as well get used to his name, looked like he was gonna be around for a while; Truman was already paying to buy him a set of new teeth. You'd think Truman would have his pick of the litter, just go around town, flinging his money left and right at any of the good-looking young boys who were killing time there, but no, he had to go and find himself the plainest-looking man/boy on God's green earth: a trucker's tan covering ropy arm muscles, the rest of him doughy as Casper the Ghost, with buck teeth that looked like something off a ventriloquist's dummy and more hair on his chest than his head. He was a "man's man," Truman kept saying; Myrtle said he sure wasn't a "woman's man," because she wouldn't look at him twice. (Another thing Myrtle said, mainly to herself: "Who can understand what goes on in the hearts of white folks?")

Maybe he *was* just there to fix the AC. Once, Myrtle went into Truman's bedroom, not realizing anybody was home, and found them both up on the bed, fully clothed and the spread not even turned down, cutting pictures out of Truman's fancy magazines. Truman invited her to hop up on the bed and help out as well, tossed some *National Geographic* at her and said, "Have at 'em." He liked to tease her by pointing out the pictures of nearly naked

African natives and saying he'd send her to the "dark continent" for a vacation one of these days. She'd say, "Now why the h-e-double-hockey-sticks would I want to go off to a damn fool country like that, where it's hotter than the blazes?" and he'd say, "Myrtle, that's where your people came from." She'd sass right back, "My people come from Enid, Oklahoma, and ain't no two ways about it."

As she and Danny cut out pictures, Truman began pasting them onto plain white paper kites he had bought, the plainer the better, to show off his homemade decorations. A man rich as Truman, gluing his own ornaments onto cheap little paper kites, cutting out letters that spelled his name, and Danny's. If you didn't know better, you'd think a child had adorned the kites; they had childish things on them: birds and bees and cats and dogs and clouds and trees and suns and moons and happy things. You wouldn't know they were the work of a big famous important author. (That's what Truman called himself, so Myrtle did, too, even though she'd never read one of his books. She tried to once, but it gave her a headache.) He said that's how he made kites when he was a child; it was good enough for then, and it was good enough for now.

His were better than anything he could buy.

But after he began calling that woman the other night, he'd started hoarding some of the cut-out pictures for something he called "top secret!" That's what he'd say with a giggle, slapping Myrtle's hand and wagging his finger at her if she tried to sort through those pictures, discern any rhyme or reason to them. Danny just accepted whatever Truman said and didn't ask questions: "top secret!" didn't scratch and fester at him like it did Myrtle. But she'd worked for Truman long enough to know that "top secret!" was really just an invite to "dig in!" so she did, first chance she had when he was out of town.

And what she found in Truman's office was as weird as any of his books.

He'd pasted the second set of pictures onto cardboard snakebite kits, which had been emptied of their razors and tubes and suction cups. The scenes he came up with seemed to have some kind of elaborate design only he understood; they sure weren't the Moon and June kinds of things he put on the kites.

No, these were scary: snakes and buzzing, preying insects; wasps with their stingers pulled out, their wings torn; tribal chiefs covered in war paint; even Hollywood stars, but cut up in strange ways. Like Fred Astaire's body—Myrtle could tell because he wore a tie for a belt—but with a raven's head instead of his own, or Grace Kelly, her face atop the long neck of a swan, but with the neck stretched out and bit in two by a snake, fangs bared, just where the box opened. Swans and snakes, he used a lot of those. If he found a snake or swan picture he liked in some magazine, he'd have Myrtle go and buy up all the copies of it she could find. It's almost like the pictures, taken together, told some kind of story, but one so bizarre you didn't want to spend much time figuring it out.

At least Myrtle J. Bennett didn't.

When she finally got up the nerve to ask Truman about them— and admit she'd been snooping—he said they were his "Garden of Earthly Delights." Myrtle didn't know what that was, but said the pictures didn't look all that delightful, and as for gardens, she pre- ferred the kind you could get something to eat out of.

Once he was finished decorating a box—Myrtle asked how he knew when he was done, and he said he just knew, just like he knew when he was finally finished writing something—he dropped it inside a clear, Plexiglas shell: a Garden of Earthly Delights encased in plastic. (Just try keeping your fingerprints off those; they were hell to keep clean.) Then he stacked them on the shelves in his studio, like something in a museum.

"So what do you do with them now?" Myrtle kept after him. "Just look at 'em? Nobody knows they're here but me, not even Mr. Danny."

"They'll know soon enough. She'll know, and she'll forgive me. She has to. Everything's counting on her," he said, as mysterious as he had been when he first started talking about his "top secret!" project.

When he got to talking like that, all Myrtle J. Bennett knew was what she didn't know, which was: who knows what goes on in the hearts of white people?

Chapter Three

On the fourth day, Nelle finally told her older sister Alice about the calls.

The two old women buttered their toast at the breakfast table, and with each ferocious, precise scrape of the knife against the bread, Alice made her feelings clear. "Nelle Harper, you know"—scrape—"I don't"—scrape—"approve." No one who knew her sister worth a lick called her Harper. They called her Nelle, or if they were family, Nelle Harper, but stretched out, southern style. Calling up and asking for "Harper" was a dead giveaway you were a stranger.

Alice put her knife down lest she start stabbing it into the air, the way she'd like to stab into Truman. "He ruined your life once; I don't want him doing it again. Ghosts indeed. I hope when I'm gone the good Lord gives me leave to come back and haunt him." Nelle had told Alice about Truman's ghosts, but not about her own. But surely Alice felt them, as well, coming for her, so much older? Two spinsters, one near the end of her life, the other gaining on her, and not telling each other their secrets.

Nelle didn't respond, just poured juice for the both of them, as she had ever since they'd moved in together. Sometimes Nelle thought it hadn't been a good idea, them living together the half of the year she lived in Monroeville instead of Manhattan, but it really had made the most sense. Except now, half the year had stretched into most of the year, as Alice needed more help getting around. Their old house, the one so many pilgrims came to find, was long gone, a soft-serve ice cream shack in its place; what were the sisters going to do, throw away good money on two separate houses when they barely needed a room each? No, the one-story brick ranch house suited them just fine, and if it meant Nelle had to contend with Alice's breakfast recitals every morning, then so be it.

Alice sipped her juice and continued. "He dumped you. You did all that work for him, he gives you *half* a dedication, then goes gallivanting on those talk shows taking all the credit . . ."

"He paid me."

"Not enough. Still makes me sick just to think about it."

"What—the murders or how little I got paid?"

That shut Alice up, but not for long. Alice never shut up for long, even as she moved into her seventies. Especially as she moved into her seventies; she'd earned the right to say anything she wanted.

"He got you when you were very tender, very vulnerable, just waiting for your own book to come out . . ."

"I have never been vulnerable a day in my . . ."

". . . that's what he always did, even as a child, he had a gift for it. Little fairy child like that, zeroing in on other people's soft spots. Imagine. You're the one got all those people to talk to him, and there he goes, adding fuel to the fire about The Book . . . telling people he . . ."

"Hush."

Alice had violated the cardinal principle: never talk about The Book.

It was the thing that hung over them like the rock of Sisyphus, teetering at the top of a hill, the merest whisper capable of sending it down to flatten them.

The Book, the thing that Nelle had labored over for years, writing and rewriting and writing again, and people still had the nerve to . . .

"Why didn't she write another one?"

"Did Truman really write it?"

Alice was sick of it. So was Nelle, she just didn't feel the need to go on and on about it. But it was the sole conversation her sister had been having, usually with herself, for the last two decades. Every year, some writer came to town—so impressed with themselves for finding their way to Podunk, Alabama— trying to dredge it all up, all over again. So impressed with them- selves, thinking they'd get the scoop, once and for all. Well, Alice was impressed with herself, too: she just handed them a pack of Xeroxes she'd already stapled up, the past interviews she or Nelle had given long ago, so they didn't need to ever give one again. The answers they'd already given were still good enough, about why Nelle had never written another book: "When you start at the top, there's nowhere else to go."

And then Alice would hand them a bill, for the cost of the copying.

She wasn't her lawyer father's daughter for nothing, carrying on the family legacy as a lawyer herself, even though she was so hard of hearing her clients practically had to shout to be heard. Not that there were many clients these days: title searches, some wills, the business of life. Mostly she was engaged in the business of protecting her sister, even though Nelle, leathery and sun-bleached, had no need for extra protection. Alice was handy with a cease and desist letter, as when the local historical society came out with *Calpurnia's Cookbook*—really, the nerve—or the local golf club wanted to name an invitational in Nelle's honor. No, thank you, Alice politely wrote back, on her sister's behalf; there's no need for that. No, thank you; they'd been brought up to be polite southern ladies, even when they were saying no. But if a second or third overture was made, that's when Alice got nasty—southern nasty, which was as nasty as you could get. "I find myself giving an interview I never agreed to in the first place," she'd say, then slam down the phone, or bang shut the door.

"No, if I would have picked up that phone first, when he called that very first night"—now Alice was shouting to Nelle, her normal decibel level, continuing the private conversation she had started in her head—"there would have been no second night to it, let alone a third."

"I thank you for defendin' my honor," Nelle said, as she got up and kissed her sister on top of the head, on her way to the icebox.

"Something's twitchin' in that little mind of yours, and I don't like it one bit," Alice said, as Nelle snuck a piece of caramel cake with burnt-sugar icing. "And while you're out—I know you're goin' somewhere, Nelle Harper, doing Lord knows what—swing by Doc Jensen's, if it's not already too late, to save those teeth of yours from rotting all the way to kingdom come and back because of all that sugar and sweet tea you guzzle."

Nelle nursed the cake in a Dixie napkin with little blue and pink baby bunnies on it and left the house, taking a big chomp out of it to coincide with the back door slamming, that simultaneous explosion of sugar and door that told her the day could begin.

Alice, who never had to leave home because her law office was there, tried one last time, calling out through the screen door, "Nothing's open this early. *Where* are you *going?* What did he *put in your head*, little sister?"

"You'll know when I do, Bear," her sister called back, some crackle in her voice for the first time in a while, a bit of sparkle through the cataract. The phone calls from Truman had put something in her head, some memory that had filtered through in bits and pieces, as dreams, during the past few nights. And she would make this rare trek out of her house, and alone, to find out what it was.

—

Truman had laughed at her in Kansas, when she insisted a Coca-Cola cake with caramel icing was the way into the hearts and minds of these midwesterners. If Truman wanted them to *spill* their guts, first he'd have to fill their guts—and no better way than with dessert. Sugar and butter would grease the wheels of this investigation.

They had been invited to Sunday supper at the home of Marie

Dewey and her husband, Alvin, who was heading the task force for the Kansas Bureau of Investigation. It was the first break they got, after Truman had nearly derailed the whole thing by cavalierly proclaiming to Alvin—upon their very first meeting, their very first meeting—that he didn't give a hoot and holler if the killer was ever caught. That wasn't his interest; his only interest was writing about the effects of murder on a small town.

Well, said Mr. Alvin Dewey, he could just hoot and holler his way back to New York City, not even stop at the hotel to pack up his bags, because his only interest was catching the killer.

Nelle had patched things over—"Oh, no, no, that's not what Truman meant, not what he meant at all, sir"—while privately she wanted to take Truman's scarf (the very scarf she had begged him not to wear unless he wanted to end up as dead as the Clutters) and pull it tight around his neck. Her apology got them an invitation to Sunday supper.

It was just a few weeks into their first trip to Kansas, while people were still sniffing around Truman. He was so nutty, maybe he was the killer, some of them probably thought. And that strange tall woman with him: was she his gun moll, Bonnie to his Clyde? Truman had packed pâté for the trip, thinking he might use it as a bribe, never thinking these people might not be interested in eating some poor animal's mashed-up liver. Nelle—smart, wise Nelle—insisted a Coca-Cola cake was the way to go; it was the way to go in Monroeville when you were trying to make an impression or meet someone new—although there was no one new in Monroeville left to meet—and it would do for Kansas just as well.

When they got to the Deweys', Nelle led the way, holding her cake aloft; Truman had insisted on taking his pâté as a backup, even though he kept it hidden in his coat. (Plus a bottle of J&B Scotch, which he kept visible, and accessible, at every moment.) Marie Dewey burst out laughing and pointed to her table: there, as its centerpiece, was the exact same thing: another Coca-Cola cake, and beside it, New Orleans–style rice and beans.

Of course, Truman insisted the cake was his idea, that he never went anywhere without it.

Especially to the home of new friends.

Which he sincerely hoped the Deweys would become.

He laid it on thicker than the fudgelike caramel icing; Nelle thought she would gag. But they did become fast, new friends, and had kept up through the years, exchanging Christmas cards and recipes and birth announcements. New friends, now old; they had remained better friends—or at least more constant—than Nelle and Truman had.

—

Nelle licked the last crumb of cake from the napkin and continued her morning constitutional into town, to the hideaway that had somehow come to her mind, ever since Truman's first call just a few nights ago.

You got what you came for, didn't you?

She stopped, midlick.

Why had that come to mind? It was a line from something she vaguely remembered, but couldn't quite place:

You got what you came for.

But who'd said it, and why?

Had she got what she'd come for?

Don't wanna go there, not this early in the morning.

She moved on, but stopped again when she suddenly remembered there was more to the line:

You got what you came for, didn't you? Then why not go?

It was something someone had said—a woman in a movie, she thought?—before panic took over.

Before a question turned to begging and pleading: then why not *go?*

She didn't remember what came after, but it wasn't good.

Had one of the Clutters said it?

She didn't know, but she sped up on her way to the hideaway, before another voice in her head made her change her mind.

Chapter Four

In the humble opinion of Myrtle J. Bennett, Truman had officially lost his marbles.

It was surprising it had taken her this long to come to that conclusion.

The late-night, drunken phone calls to that woman hadn't convinced her, Myrtle having to dig up his ancient address books, then keep herself awake so she could hang up the phone after Truman passed out with it in his hand.

Nor had his insistence that Myrtle start placing the orders for his snakebite kits—in her name, the very same name the good Lord gave her—from some new place deep over the border in Mexico. He didn't want his "top secret!" getting out.

No, now he'd started mailing off the damn things. It wasn't enough that she had to look at them as she dusted; now he was going to inflict those cubes of plastic and cardboard and bizarre pasted pictures on the rest of the world. Oh, he never told her, but she knew. He'd come home from mysterious errands that he wouldn't explain, muttering that this was finally going to make it all right, this was finally getting his juices going again, and she'd find his pockets stuffed full of mail slips. She'd find his wastepaper baskets overflowing with snippets of wrapping paper. She'd see gaps where the boxes used to be on display in his office. She'd find heads and things cut out of her favorite magazines, just when she'd settle down on the couch with them for her coffee break.

And he wouldn't explain any of it, just get nervous and jittery and say, "I've gotta get this out before I go; I don't have much time left."

When Myrtle asked what he meant—"Time left for what?"—he'd snap that he would have hired somebody from Busybodies Anonymous instead of the local Luby's Cafeteria, where he'd found Myrtle, if he'd wanted to answer that.

His fingers would be covered with dried glue from working on the boxes, and he'd rub together the now smooth fingerprints and say, "They'll never find it now."

But find what, he wouldn't say.

And then, one day, the coup de grâce (that was the fancy French term Truman used; Myrtle didn't know what it meant, but she figured out a rough translation: "Now he's gone really crazy").

He wanted to go kite flying in the middle of the Palm Springs desert.

"Why?" she asked.

"So I can get my message up in the air, closer to God," he said. "I'll spell it out on a kite; that way He'll *have* to read it."

"And just what message do you have for our Lord and Savior?" she asked.

"Top secret!" he cackled, then slapped her hand.

These days, whenever Truman said, "Go fly a kite," he meant it.

—

As the day of the kite flying got closer—Truman had been watching the weather reports like a hawk, trying to figure out when they'd have enough wind to launch—he said he'd had a change of plan.

It wasn't a message to God he wanted to send, but to Nancy Clutter. She was the one he wanted "*off his back.*" That's the way he said it, like it was underlined.

God could wait.

For some reason, he wasn't as secretive about his message to Nancy: it would read *I'm Sorry*. Myrtle felt like telling him the same message would work just fine for God, but decided to keep her mouth shut for once.

But when she asked him, "Sorry for what? Who's Nancy Clutter?" he wouldn't answer, just complained, "Haven't you ever read a damn book in your whole life?"

It was one of the few tiffs they'd ever had.

"I've gotta take care of the two of them; get Nancy out of the way, before I can really focus on Nelle. It would take years to explain, and I don't have years left. I don't have any time left. Everything's crowding my brain too much and too fast . . ."

Myrtle's, too. She didn't have a clue what he was talking about.

On brightly colored pages torn from magazines, Truman traced out the massive letters himself, saying he couldn't find them "store-bought and big enough to get my point across." He rambled on that it was Nancy's brother Kenyon who was blind as a bat and really needed the extra-large letters, but he wasn't "ON MY BACK!" the way Nancy was.

Truman's hands shook as he cut around his tracings, so Myrtle took over, afraid he'd cut himself and get the letters all crooked at the same time. If he was going to do a damn fool project like this, he might as well do it right. Like she always said, "Who knows what goes on in the hearts of white folks?" That's what she felt like gluing on a kite, for all the world to see.

Sometimes, if she fixed him another drink—or he fixed him-self one, going into the kitchen for his "orange drink" that was 90 percent vodka, with a splash of pulp from an orange grown on his own property—the shaking would die down, and he could return to the cutting. Sometimes, Myrtle would put her hands over Truman's as he cut, guiding him, and she felt the same silent happiness he seemed to.

It gave him something to do.

It gave them all something to do, since Mr. Danny and Myrtle had been drafted for the kite-flying project as well. They would all be needed to get Truman's full message across; he said there wasn't room enough on just one kite. After Truman's kite with the words "I'm sorry," Mr. Danny's kite would launch the word "Forgive," and Myrtle's would bring up the rear with "Me."

Personally, she would have preferred a bigger word, something a little more elaborate, or at least a few more little ones bunched up together. She felt selfish and embarrassed singling herself out with the word "me." She argued for a "please" in there somewhere—why not on her kite? she had plenty of extra room—but Truman told her it was his message, not hers; besides, he'd gone through life doing just fine with the word "me," and look where it had gotten him.

My point exactly, Myrtle wanted to say. Look where it got you. Hiding out under a palm tree in Palm Springs, after everybody in the world deserted you, slaving away on a pile of pages you call your "magnum opus." Sometimes he called it his "payback to the bitches." Myrtle didn't like when he talked like that; not because she minded a little cussing now and then, she just wondered if she was one of the bitches.

So all told, "I'm sorry. Forgive me," became Truman's final message to Nancy Clutter.

"I'm sorry. Forgive me."

That was it: simple, clean, declarative sentences, nothing more, nothing less.

Nancy could take it or leave it.

And that was the end of that.

Almost.

Now that Truman knew *what* he wanted to say, he had to decide *where* to say it: should the cut-out letters go on the top side of the kites, or underneath? Although really, Myrtle argued, with the wind whipping them every which way but loose, was there a true top or bottom? Truman said that very question had perplexed him his entire life, then giggled; Myrtle didn't know what he was talking about.

On top, Truman finally decided; whether or not *he* could see the words, as they rattled above him, *Nancy* could, and that's what mattered. She'd be looking down on them, from heaven. Besides, Truman said, he didn't want anyone down on the ground looking up at the kites and thinking the people holding them were crazy. No, Myrtle thought to herself—they'll just see you and Mr. Danny and big fat me running across the desert, about to give ourselves strokes in the heat; they won't need to see anything else to know we're crazy.

As the final assembly began taking place—Truman shredding his fine French bed sheets into tiny little strips for tails on the kites—Myrtle had a brainstorm that almost derailed the whole project.

Since they were going to the trouble of getting the kites up and everything, why not kill two birds with one stone and launch her maid service at the same time? Truman had been promising it forever, and she wasn't getting any younger; she'd have her own fleet of girls to do the work, and she could finally put her feet up for once. They could put her name on the underside of the kites, since that part was just going to waste; it was prime real estate. She wanted the name to be Myrtle's Maids, but Truman insisted on Myrtle Bennett Inc.—it had to be classy or he wouldn't have anything to do with it. She said first name or last, it really didn't matter; she just wanted her name up in the sky, big and black, like her.

No, Truman said; one message at a time. He didn't want to confuse the reader, whether it was Nancy Clutter or someone who needed to have their windows and washing done. There was a time, and place, for everything. After so many years with Truman, Myrtle knew not to press things, until her boss threw this curveball at her:

"Besides, have you figured out how to get blood off baseboards? Any girl can't do that, you shouldn't hire her. That's the real test; you figure out how to do that, then I'll launch your maid service."

And he sucked in his cheeks and raised his eyebrows, moistened his lips with his tongue, silently daring Myrtle to take the bait.

She did.

"What the heck are you talkin' about?"

"Just ask Nancy Clutter about blood on the baseboards" was all he would say.

Now Myrtle was really confused: had Nancy Clutter been somebody's maid?

—

The Day of the Kites finally arrived.

Truman made Mr. Danny and Myrtle each put on one of the sun hats he kept on his wall for decoration. Mr. Danny took one look in the mirror and said he looked ridiculous, wearing a lady's floppy hat out into the desert, but Truman said Danny was the one who needed it most, being as how he was just three wisps of hair short of a sunstroke. Mr. Danny said he was an air conditioner man for a reason; he didn't like being outdoors.

Truman said, did he like being all alone?

That shut him up.

He put on the hat.

Truman had Myrtle fix a picnic lunch to take with them, fried chicken and potato salad and cornbread, and several thermoses of his "orange drink." He didn't know how long they'd be gone, and he didn't want them to get hungry, or thirsty, while they waited.

"Waited for what?" Myrtle asked.

"A sign from Nancy, that she's read the message."

A sign from Nancy that the hauntings were over, Truman thought to himself, so he could move on to the even more important task with

Nelle. It had come to his mind the first night he called her, after their long silence; he just regretted he hadn't thought of it sooner.

It would be his final act of contrition, and it would take every last ounce of thinking and planning he had.

They didn't have far to go to get to the desert. Just throw a stick in any direction in Palm Springs and you'd find one; the whole town was a desert, just flats and baked earth and an occasional palm tree or cactus sticking out. The landscape was dotted with steams and springs and mud baths that Truman would cover himself with, saying it was to stay fit, but Myrtle wondered how healthy that really was: wallow in mud that other people—other *strangers*—had already sat in? Heated mud?

"That's the point," Truman said. "It sweats out the poisons."

"You wanna sweat out the poison, leave your 'orange drink' at home."

It was the same argument they had day and night, and now they were having it again. If he wanted to go traipsing up and down the desert, trying to get a kite up in the air, then he'd better not be all liquored up. He'd take a few steps in this sun and keel over.

He looked at Myrtle. "Maybe you can get it up."

He said it in all innocence.

"Don't look at me," she said, "I figure Mr. Danny's the one to 'get it up.'"

Together, she and Truman giggled; together, they turned to look at Mr. Danny.

Before he could say a word, Truman fixed him with a stare and said, "You want to be fixing ACs the rest of your life? Then start running."

Start running he did and didn't stop, catching the updraft and handing the kites off, one by one, to Truman and Myrtle.

She looked up in the sky and saw their three kites whipping in the wind, pulling taut against their strings and making a sound like they were trying to escape. They trailed one behind the other like the Niña, the Pinta, and the Santa Maria, with Truman guiding their course like Christopher Columbus on his way to a new land.

I'm Sorry . . .

Forgive . . .

Me . . .

Majestic white canvases, with a message of apology shimmering against a cloudless blue sky. A whiplash of paper, and fine French bed linen.

Myrtle looked at Truman as he looked up at his fleet: he wasn't an old man anymore, heaving and panting and sweating beet red, but a child.

She'd never seen him so happy.

"Nancy, do you see?! It's all for you . . . it's working! I told you!"

But the happiness didn't last long. It never did.

The wind began to flag, and the kites to droop.

Myrtle's first thought: Look quick, Nancy, whoever you are, we can't keep these up for long.

Her second thought: Damn. There goes some prime advertising space.

Truman began yelling at Mr. Danny, "Start running! Grab the kites and run! We got to keep them up! She hasn't answered yet!"

His words echoed in the desert, up to the sky and back.

Danny took a last belt from the thermos, wiped a shirtsleeve of sweat off his face, and began running yet again—Truman was right, he didn't want to be fixing ACs the rest of his life—until he stumbled across something and fell flat on the desert floor.

His fall pulled the first kite down with him; "I'm sorry"

crashed onto a rock; "Forgive" and "Me" flew away, somewhere over Palm Springs.

Truman reached down to Mr. Danny, not to help him up, but to scream at him some more: "You idiot! Now they're all gone! We'll have to start all over! You didn't give her a chance . . ."

But what he saw on the ground silenced him.

The only sound was "I'm sorry," thrashing against the rocks.

Mr. Danny had tripped over a snake carcass, big and plump and sad and dead. It was a green Mojave diamondback rattler, shorter than most, and thus female; Truman had been bitten by a snake as a child and almost died, so he knew his snakes. It was gray-green, the gray now overtaking the scales on its back because it was dead. Curled into a ball, but with its triangular head jutting out, it looked as if it had been trying to escape when it sensed footsteps. Jutting its head out, ready to run, it had been shot, just like Nancy Clutter.

Truman fell to his knees and crossed himself.

It was the sign he had been waiting for.

Nancy had answered.

There was no other way to interpret it.

"OhJesusGod, ohJesusLord, now I can sleep, now I can rest, now I can finish what I started with Nelle," Truman said, crying so quietly you could barely hear it.

Myrtle cried, too, loud enough for everybody to hear it: "Now I can sleep with that damn ghost gone! And good riddance to bad rubbish!"

They'd gotten what they'd come for: a sign from Nancy. She was letting them know she'd heard their prayers, and this was her answer:

They could go home, and move on to Nelle.

Chapter Five

Last night, Nelle dreamed about the tree.

It filled the entire perimeter of her brain, nothing but bark and long, groaning branches and leaves in their sad transition from summer to fall. In the one part of the dream she could remember—she thought it must be near the end, but she had no clue what had come before—she felt her hand desperately reaching up for the squirrel hole she knew was there, just above her fingertips. But even though she was her current age in the dream, and taller by a good foot or two than the child who had originally stood on tippy-toes to look inside, she still couldn't reach it.

But just when she was about to give up, her forearm magically extended and began to snake its way into the receptacle. Now, height wasn't the problem, girth was: her big meaty hand was just too big to get inside. As she tried to force the fit, stabbing her fist at a shape that refused to give, the bark around the hole scratched at her flesh—that mound where her thumb and index finger circled together, her knobby, arthritic knuckles, and the side of her little pinky, all by its lonesome. Those areas bore the brunt of the old chinaberry's roughness, as she continued her square-peg assault on the round hole, and thus it was a complete mystery to her—and no mystery at all—that she woke up with her hand scratched white, the layers of suntanned skin scraped off to reveal ashy pink underneath. These days, there was very little separation between day and night, between dream and doing.

She had probably just clawed at herself during the night, in sympathy with the frustrated dream-woman who couldn't get what she wanted; she wasn't about to begin thinking she had actually risen from her sleep to visit the tree.

How could she?

It wasn't there anymore.

The tree had been chopped down when the old house was sold, and the lot turned into Mel's Dairy Dream. She wasn't a sentimental woman, but she had taken a small branch from the tree when the ax hit its trunk; she kept it, still, underneath her bed. She heard someone else in town bragged about having "a piece of that tree" from The Book; it was God's tree, anyone had a right to it, but still, that didn't sit quite right with her. The practical side of her said she could use the limb on an intruder; the other side of her wondered why there was a tree branch tucked under the bed whenever the vacuum cleaner hit it. But other than that—and how often did she actually clean under the bed?—she rarely thought about the tree. That is, until now, when the dream brought it back to her for the first time in years.

Now, she was on her way to see it—a tree that was no longer there, just as her mind was no longer there. It had snapped the minute the equally crazy Truman had said, "You'll know what to do. You'll know where I'm sending it." She didn't know *what* he was sending, but *where*—their old tree house was the one and only place he could have meant, even if it wasn't there anymore. It had been so long since Truman had come to town he wouldn't know it had been torn down. That's why she hadn't told Alice where she was going; as much as Alice loved her, she would have been on the phone to the men in white jackets the minute Nelle let the screen door slam behind her.

It was up in that tree, in the backyard of the old Lee house, that she and Truman had first become writers. Each of them provided an essential ingredient (besides imagination and loneliness): Nelle, a beat-up old Underwood typewriter that her father had donated to the cause, and Truman, a waterlogged Webster's dictionary that he carried everywhere, practically bowed down by its weight. It was his pride and joy, as precious and crucial to him as a teddy bear might have been to another needy child. Remembering that, Nelle had to stop and catch her breath: maybe it was the sugar overload of the caramel cake, so early in the morning, but more likely, it was the memory of a six-year-old boy whose best friend was someone's discarded dictionary. The memory of a child who loved words so much, he slept with them under his pillow so they would burrow into his head at night: it took her very breath away.

It was up in that tree house—reached by a few weather-beaten boards and the squirrel's hole that served as an extra foothold—that she and Truman swore, whatever happened to them, they would always stay together. (The heartbreak of a child, at six years old, already knowing that change would come, and making plans for the future. He knew, even then; she didn't. That took her breath away, too.) They swore a promise of forever and a day, on blood they'd let from their little fingers. Nelle used the Swiss Army knife she'd stolen from her brother Ed to break the skin; she went first, poking at the tip of the index finger on her left hand. She even sucked at it to get more of a flow going. She had to keep sucking so it wouldn't dry up during the five or six tries it took before she struck gold with Truman; he kept pulling his finger away at the last second, so it was sliced up, like the gills on a fish.

There had been no thought of him pricking his own finger; he kept his eyes clinched shut during the whole process, until she told him it was safe to open them and look. At that, he'd become wide-eyed and mesmerized, as if he had expected his own blood to run blue, just as it looked under the surface of his albino white skin. And the sight of that blood shook something loose, something unafraid and inspired, in him: he immediately spit into the mixture and told Nelle to do the same; that's what made true blood brothers, he'd read in Huck Finn. He roughly jammed his index finger onto hers and ground them together, as if he knew he had to do it fast or else he'd change his mind and go get himself cleaned up.

And it was in that same tree that Boo Radley had been born.

That took her breath away, too.

For the third time on this morning sojourn, she had to put out her hand on a neighbor's mailbox to steady herself.

—

His real name was Son Boular, and even as children—especially as children—they had known he was different. Nelle and Truman thinking somebody *else* was different; that was rich. Nelle smiled at the thought now, a sad smile, on her way to the tree.

Son, already in high school when Nelle and Truman were just children, lived a few doors down from them, and never came out of his house except at night. That was the result, it was whispered, of a bargain his father had made with the local judge to keep Son from being sent to jail after his teenage high jinks got out of hand. It was also whispered that, under the cover of darkness, he killed and ate neighborhood cats for sustenance and peeped in windows, for a different kind of sustenance. Of course, Truman and Nelle had never seen any of these nocturnal actions; they had never seen Son at all, except for once, at a party that had almost been the end of them all.

Truman, seven years old at the time, had decided to throw a good-bye party for himself, the likes of which the people of Monroeville would never forget. Lillie Mae Faulk, his flighty mother, had gotten remarried in New York, and was bringing him north to live with her; this party would be the farewell to end all farewells. It would fall on Halloween, Truman's favorite holiday, and costumes would be required as the price of admission. He and Nelle spent weeks planning their outfits: she would come as Tom Swift, her favorite literary hero, in a pair of overalls that were no different from those she wore all the time, and Truman would do himself up as Fu Manchu, complete with yellow makeup and a skinny black pigtail he braided from a pair of his cousin Bud's dark silk socks. Of course, a dangling pigtail on Truman was an open invitation that said "Snatch Me," even if he was the party's host, but that would come later.

Buddy's dark delicates weren't the only familial contribution: Truman's gentle cousin Sook—at seventy more childlike than Truman was at seven—would make one of her famous fruitcakes a month or so earlier than usual, as well as elderberry lemonade to be served in a cut-glass punch bowl; his cousin Jennie, the stern, humorless head of the household, would make divinity and cobbler—or instruct the cook to make it; and Jennie's younger sister Callie—pulled away from teaching to help run the family millinery business, and bitter the rest of her life because of it—would be drafted to keep the Victrola cranked up all evening long, pulled as close as it would go to a back window inside the house, so music would spill out into the yard. Sook, who lived for Truman, would even sacrifice a bushel of the apples she'd ordered special from up North, for apple bobbing in the old washtub.

The likely reason Truman's relatives were so accommodating was that they already knew the heartache that awaited him in New York. Going to live with his mother was all Truman pined for, but she was as likely to send him back on the first train as keep him. Lillie Mae—who'd now christened herself Nina, in preparation for the sophisticated new life she hoped for—was full of quicksilver ideas and spontaneous enthusiasms, but working a strange, delicate child like Truman into her new marriage was a little too spontaneous, to hell with guilt and good intentions. Anybody could have told her that. So if a party made Truman happy, at least for a while, then the relatives would give him the party he wanted, one he'd never forget. If they cried a little during the party, then they'd be quick not to let Truman see. If the yellow watercolor it took to turn his face into a Chinaman's rubbed off on everybody's nice clothes, then so be it.

But the real trouble wasn't Lillie Mae, it was Old John, one of the Negro field hands who'd been drafted to watch over the apple bobbing. Truman insisted he wear an all-white suit—another item of clothing filched from cousin Bud—so his jet black skin would blend into the night sky and make him appear to be headless. The guests would see just the white suit, and the starched white collar of his shirt inside it, bobbing up and down every time he swallowed, like the apples. Old John was so proud at having been invited to Mr. Truman's party—even if it was, essentially, to work at it—that he blabbed about his invitation far and wide. Too wide. The Klan heard, and decided to storm the proceedings in protest, with or without invitations.

Ah, yes; a party in Monroeville, Alabama—in the thick of the Depression and the Scottsboro Boys trial.

A party Monroeville would never forget.

For a time, it was going along just swell. Children lined up for rides on a giant toy airplane that was the lone contribution of Truman's missing-in-parental-action father, a long-distance gift from where he lived in New Orleans. The other men of the neighborhood pulled the metal-and-wood contraption up a ramp, then let it "fly" back down, a distance of all of three feet that seemed like three hundred feet to the flyers, who were more than willing to suspend their disbelief.

They were also willing to play make-believe—and squeal even more—as they touched the dead man's body parts Truman had selected and laid out with such delicacy: peeled grapes for his eyeballs, cold spaghetti for his innards. Even the grown-ups temporarily forgot the Depression, as they played Rook and sipped from the occasional flask, even stood in line for airplane rides themselves, when a scream came from the front of the house.

It was Sally Boular, yelling her head off that the Klan had her baby brother.

Everyone raced around to the front, fastest of all Nelle's daddy, Amasa, to see the Klan done up in their own Halloween costumes, ones that were all too familiar. In their white robes and peaked hoods, they had surrounded some strange and exotic creature who was trying to escape. For once, the strange and exotic creature wasn't Truman, but someone else—dressed up like a robot or an alien, crash-landed on this planet, and covered in cardboard boxes that had been strung together and painted silver. The Klan assumed it was a Negro, disguised for the party and emboldened by Old John's presence.

Amasa Lee strode through the Klansmen, knocking their torches left and right, and yanked the top box off the head of the spaceman: underneath was the sweaty, shaggy-haired face of Son Boular, wild and scared—a shy young man who just wanted to be part of the dance for once. He made what sounded like the cry of a crow—caw, caw—as he tried to beat his wings and fly away, pecking at Amasa in his terror.

Thereafter, his nickname would be "Caw"—but this only from strangers, because no one who heard him that night ever dared to make fun of the unearthly and desperate sound they had heard.

They hadn't known a human could make a sound like that.

They hadn't known a sister could make a sound like that, begging for help for a brother the rest of the town had shunned or, worse yet, forgotten.

Son's eyes were wide and petrified, as were Sally's, while Nelle's daddy tried to calm him down and lead him back to his own house, his silver robot boxes dragging behind. Sally, a few years older, tried to cover his face with her Halloween witch's cape, much as she might cover a bird's cage with a dark cloth, to calm and soothe its squawking inhabitant. Her movements were practiced and careful, loving but sad, it was a gesture she had clearly performed many times before, and would perform many times again.

Nelle and Truman followed every step of the way.

Amasa Lee promised the Boular children he'd bring over refreshments from the party, but did not extend the same offer to the Klan. Instead, he asked if they were in the business of terrorizing poor innocent white children, or any other children, for that matter. They skulked away after that, their sheets dragging in the red dirt road in front of Truman's house; they'd never get the red out of those sheets, Miss Jennie had proclaimed. You could tell who they were by what was hanging on their clothesline; serves 'em right!

In this case, all would not come out in the wash.

The party died down soon afterward—not even Truman could compete with an appearance by the Klan—and as the grown-ups began cleaning up, Nelle and Truman disappeared into their tree house. Looking down, they aimlessly pelted the ground with chinaberry bombs; they watched Old John stuff leftover apples, autographed with teeth marks, into his pockets; they watched Sook leave nibbles of fruitcake in the bushes for the neighborhood creatures.

Nelle and Truman should have known this was their time to say good-bye—he would be leaving by train the very next day—but they didn't; maybe they couldn't bring themselves to say good-bye to childhood so soon.

They talked, instead, of Sally and Son Boular, brother and sister, and of how they—Truman and Nelle—were more like that than mere next-door neighbors. They talked of how alive Son's eyes had been, at what must have seemed like his near death at the hands of the Klan, of how much sweat had poured off his face. His heart must have been racing like a stoked-up furnace to provide that much heat; they had never seen so much sweat come off one person, and that included the field hands. Truman took a broader, more adult, more selfish view of things: he said they had just seen history being made: the night the Klan lost power in town. Not just witnessed it, *caused* it: it was all because of him and his party.

Truman had made history, in other words.

At eight years old.

Nelle could have answered by saying her father was the one who had made history by shaming the Klan. But she remained silent, letting Truman have his triumph as a parting gift. (Maybe that was her good-bye to him after all.) She was already thinking of a different kind of history: looking into the future, and knowing she would never forget the terrified face of Son Boular as long as she lived. That would be the last time she would ever see his face, terrified or otherwise; he would die of pneumonia when he was just thirty years old, never having come out of his house again, as far as she knew, until he was given a final ride— to the town cemetery.

The night the Klan was destroyed in Monroeville.

The night Boo Radley was born.

The night she and Truman said their first and hardest good-bye, without words.

They were all one and the same.

Without thinking, Truman unhooked the Chinaman's pigtail from the back of his head and put it in Nelle's hand.

Maybe that was his gift to her; she had it still.

—

Nelle picked up her pace, trying to outrace those memories and get to the place where they had started, all at once.

By now, she had convinced herself that her dream had been a prophecy: something from Truman would be waiting there, at the place where the tree had originally stood. That tree had been their Rosetta stone, and Truman her Merlin: he'd figure out a way to make the tree reappear if anyone could.

But no, nothing was there—not a tree, magically resprouted during the night, and certainly not a package with her name on it. Is that what old age would be? Waiting for packages that never came?

No, all that was there was a gravel-filled parking lot, some carved-up picnic tables etched with the names of boyfriends and girlfriends and who wanted to do what to whom, very little of which had to do with love, and the smelly dumpster behind Mel's Dairy Dream, overflowing with empty ice cream buckets and buzzing with shiny green flies, drunk on sugar and cream.

That's what her childhood, and the house in which she had grown up, had come to.

She had to get away before she gagged.

Maybe it was disappointment about to make her sick; she'd been so certain. (Certain of what? That she'd lost her mind? That Truman had addressed a bulky envelope to "the third chinaberry from the left" and that the local mailman had actually delivered it, tucking it away in a squirrel's cubbyhole?)

But then again, she got everything else people sent, with barely an address, so why not get something in a tree? Sometimes she wished the postal service would just shut down; it wouldn't leave her alone. The letters she got: it was their favorite book, they were her number one fan, wouldn't she please write back, please accept this prize, please honor us with a few words, please do this, please do that—she knew how Santa Claus must have felt, the demand for toys blurring his eyesight and shredding his fingertips with paper cuts.

Mostly, she got copies of The Book that people wanted her to autograph, with return envelopes, postage included. She always signed and returned them; she could hardly ignore the readers who went to the trouble and expense of sending stamps—and often the choice of stamp was just as careful and revealing as the composition of the letter inside. It was always something noble and lyrical—not enough just to be a plain old American flag— the stamps had to picture a bird in midflight, or a black man holding his trembling young daughter's hand. Lately, though, she'd been hearing that those very fans were selling their autographed copies of The Book; that was enough to make her never sign anything again, no matter how pretty or plentiful the stamps.

Some of the letters were more clever than others, and those she did give an extra five minutes of her time—because, truth to tell, what else did she have but time? Those were the packages that came with little soap-bar carvings of figures, jacks and cat's-eye marbles, nubbed-down crayons in the colors of childhood.

Those were the geegaws Boo Radley had left in the tree for

Scout and Jem, although, in reality, nobody had left anything for anybody there. She'd made it all up, even though, as a child, she'd never given up hope that something would magically appear there. It was the perfect secret hiding place; her childhood was made up of the yearning for such secret hiding places.

She used to stand on her tiptoes and peer inside the hole at least twice a day, on her way to and from school. When she confessed her secret yearning to Amasa, he told her she'd better be careful or a squirrel would jump out and bite her on the nose and she'd have to get rabies shots. When she reported this back to Truman, he added the detail that she'd likely start foaming at the mouth first, to give everybody fair warning; the only cure was to be tied down and get shots in the stomach, which was considered by some to be worse than the disease itself. Out of his love for her, he'd overcome his squeamishness to help hold her down—if it came to that.

Years later, living in a cold-water walk-up in New York and struggling to write out the story of her childhood, she'd told friends her fantasy about a squirrel's hidey-hole becoming her own private Horn of Plenty. They'd smiled and said nothing more; Michael and Joy were a creative and artistic couple who had children of their own; they knew the imaginations of children, and knew better than to squelch them.

That same year, Nelle had visited their palatial apartment in New York, rather than stay in her hovel, for Christmas. Money was tight; she made a pittance as a reservations clerk for British Airlines, and her father was sick, no longer able to send her much to help out. She'd made stockings with felt and glitter for the children, and written a poem for their parents; she hadn't expected anything in return, except the pleasure of their company. The wrapping paper that flew off presents and into the air inside the apartment would take the place of snow that had not come outside, as it had rarely come in Alabama.

But none of that wrapping paper had come from presents to Nelle.

She smiled anyway; Christmas was a time for children, not needy adults. But as soon as the little ones finished opening their gifts—their parents had had a good year, and spoiled them with too much—Nelle got up to begin laying out the Christmas lunch she had helped prepare. She was glad for an excuse to leave the room; she didn't want them to see the expression on her face. They were so good to her, but she was homesick, and tired of working so hard: all day smiling for the public, all night digging into her soul and putting it down on paper, with little to show for either.

She heard a giggle and turned around on her way to the kitchen. Michael and Joy looked at her expectantly: do you think we forgot you, our best friend? O ye of little faith. Look inside the tree.

Even the children giggled, in on the secret.

Nelle went to the tree and looked past the colored ornaments and twinkling fairy lights into its branches: there, deep inside, propped up on a branch that was eye level, was an envelope with her name on it.

She turned around and gave the couple a puzzled look; the children gave another giggle, even a clap. Their surprise had come off after all.

She reached into the branches, needles and sap prickling her skin, and pulled out the envelope.

Tucked inside was a card the children had made, construction paper decorated with green and red crayon and tufts of cotton.

Inside that was a check, made out to Nelle, the amount large enough to live on for a year.

The year she needed to finish her book.

It had not yet become The Book.

The year she needed to prove, once and for all, or forever hold her peace, that she was a writer, like her friend Truman.

She didn't understand, or rather, she did, she just couldn't believe it—and she certainly couldn't accept it.

Joy spoke first: they wanted her to leave her job at the airline and just write. They believed in her, even though they had barely read word one of anything she had ever committed to paper, not for lack of trying. They kept asking; Nelle kept begging off, too nervous and insecure. She wanted it perfect before she showed the world, and perfect was hard to come by.

Michael said he'd had a good year with his composing, and the stock market, and Nelle Harper was a new investment he wanted to make.

Together, they wanted to make her childhood fantasy come true: they wanted her to find something good in the branches of a tree.

She refused the money, of course, as they had known she would. They continued that little charade for about ten minutes— as they'd known she would as well—and then, finally, she consented to a slight alteration: she would accept the money, but only as a loan.

One day, she would pay them back.

How, she had no earthly idea.

That was the second night Boo Radley was born.

—

Alice was waiting for Nelle on the porch, holding a brown paper-wrapped package that had already been opened.

She looked scared, almost like she was waiting for an answer of some sort.

And Alice Lee was never without an answer.

Nelle was still thinking about trees: trees that weren't there, and trees that were, bearing strange and wonderful fruit, so it took her a second to go on alert, to see what was behind Alice's expression.

Alice didn't say anything as Nelle came up the steps, just handed over the nest of torn paper and cardboard. Nelle didn't mind that she'd already opened whatever it was; that practice had begun years ago, when Nelle received the only piece of hate mail she'd ever gotten. It was a dead mockingbird; Alice had been the first to open the box and see it, just seconds before she'd swept it off the front table with a scream and baptized herself with a spray of upchuck. Ever since then, she'd felt it was her duty to open large packages and save her sister from anything unpleasant. This—whatever this was—certainly belonged in the unpleasant category.

It hadn't been mailed; there were no stamps on it, Alice had just found it waiting for them on the front porch. And it contained no dead mockingbird, but it was hard to tell what it was, or if it was better or worse than something dead. It was a small cardboard box, covered with pictures of—what? She could barely focus on what they were, there were so many shiny, competing images going on, and the glare from the midmorning sun turned them all the same blinding white. Nelle had to shade her eyes with one hand, then hold the package out a good arm's length with the other to try and make sense of it all.

They were pictures of her, taken almost twenty-five years ago, just after The Book had come out. They had appeared in a two-page article in one of the leading pictorial magazines of the day, one of the last times Nelle had knowingly allowed herself to be committed to film.

In one of the pictures, she sat in the balcony of the courthouse where her father had tried his cases, smiling at the camera as it peeped over her shoulder to the judge's bench below. In another, she walked through the playground of her youth, wearing jeans and sneakers that might have befitted a child, but certainly not a famous lady authoress, as the article stated she was primed to become. The photographer must have realized that as soon as she peeped in the boarded-up window of an old abandoned house wearing a dress.

She looked at that picture and remembered lying to the photographer, taking him to a deserted house that was not the Boulars', when he said he wanted to go to "the haunted house in the book." It was clear he hadn't read "the book"; the house wasn't haunted, by anything more than a child's overheated imagination—and a gentle giant she had created, and christened Boo Radley. Better late than never; Nelle wanted to spare that family any more pain by turning their home into a souvenir-seekers' landmark. She hurried over the thought that her book might have caused some of that pain in the first place. The lawsuit they had threatened was one thing, which she'd wiggled out of with an "Oh, it's all fiction." The looks she would get from Sally in the years to come, after Son's death, were quite another. Wasn't it enough that she had given life, and quiet, halting dignity, to someone the world would never have known without her? No, not even that was enough for Sally. Nelle had made her peace and moved on; Sally never had, long after the rest of her family had died off or moved away.

Looking at the strange box in her hand was better than remembering that. Nelle shook her head, almost trying to shake that memory away, and refocused on the pictures from the magazine: in her favorite of the bunch, she and her father sat on the porch of their old house in side-by-side rockers. Even sick and no longer able to work, Amasa had worn a dark suit and tie; it was the last picture ever taken of him.

But the photograph that haunted her most was the last one that had been shot, and the last one of the article. It was placed at the bottom of the second and final page, like a period that ended a sentence: Nelle was in her father's law office, her shirtsleeves rolled up, pages and pages scattered around her. "Working on her next novel," the caption read. She couldn't see what was on any of those pages, and her memory didn't help: were they mere props, or the real thing?

Looking at that picture again, pasted onto this strange box in her hand, knocked the breath out of her; she fell back into a chair on the porch.

It was her life, her past, staring her in the face.

"I'm calling the police," Alice announced.

"And tellin' 'em what? That some cardboard and cut-up pictures made me a little light-headed? I think not, Sister Bear."

But maybe they should call the police: Nelle felt as if she had just been robbed, and her life was what had been stolen away and glued onto a box that had snakes printed on it.

"Who sent it? Who put it here?" Alice asked.

There was no return address or name on the package, just an inevitable sense that it had been waiting, and had found its intended victim.

But there was more, besides that air of expectancy. Something else, something real and tangible, inside the box. Nelle felt its weight, heard something hitting the sides when she shook it.

She held up a finger to silence Alice, then opened the lid, afraid of what might pop out.

Alice gripped the offered finger.

Inside was a tiny coffin; there was no other way to describe it. It was made of balsa wood, the kind used to make model airplanes, and shaped like a flat sarcophagus, like something an Egyptian mummy would come in: about three-fourths of it flanged out, then the last quarter reversed that shape and started heading back in the other direction. It was plain and unpainted, not even varnished, but it had been solidly made, with the tiniest of hinges on one side, so you could open the lid.

Nelle opened the lid and was assaulted by a loamy smell: a thin layer of freshly turned earth. And crawling in it, poking its head up when the darkness was disturbed: a lone earthworm, now as terrified as Nelle.

She jerked; the whole contraption flew out of her hands and landed in the flower bed that bordered the porch.

"That does it. Now I *am* calling the police," Alice said, then went inside the house.

This time, Nelle made no move to stop her, but stepped off the porch, holding onto the guardrail for balance as she reached down between the scuppernong grape plants Alice had climbing up thin wooden stakes. The escaping earthworm dove for cover as Nelle's pinching fingers navigated down and retrieved what Alice hadn't seen, what Nelle herself had barely had time to glimpse before the box took its header:

Two other photographs, rolled together, planted in the soil at the bottom of the coffin.

Nelle picked them up and brushed the dirt off as she returned to her rocker on the porch.

Two photos.

She narrowed her eyes to see through the smudged bifocal part of her glasses. She needed a new prescription; smudge was going to make it even worse. And she needed vision right now.

One of the photos was from long ago, the other of a much more recent vintage, but she had no clue who had taken either one of them, or what—exactly—they meant.

The one on top wasn't a reproduction or page torn from a magazine, but an original she had never seen before, from long ago. In it, she and Truman were in the basement of the Clutters' house. It had been cold; they were wearing winter coats, and in their expressions it was clear they had been caught off guard; their faces were blurred as they turned to look at something outside the frame of the picture. (Maybe the blurring was their breath coming out in the chilly air; maybe it was a ghost trapped in the room.) Behind them was a single lightbulb hanging from the ceiling; it exposed the wooden stairs leading to the basement and its bare, cinderblock walls.

She remembered being down there and shuddered.

She moved the second picture on top.

It had been taken just a few weeks ago, the last time she had gone to the cemetery where her parents and brother Ed were buried, where an unwanted plot waited for her. She went every few weeks, to deliver fresh flowers, to clean out the old ones from their swampy Mason jars. Her visits there weren't a secret; they were one of her regular stops, same as Hardee's or one of the diners in town. But this photograph made it seem as if there was something secretive or furtive, or even shameful, about it, and someone was exposing her as she bent over, pulling stray weeds from Ed's grave. It was broad daylight—anybody could have taken the picture—but the very fact that they had, without her knowing it, catching her unaware like that and with some evident purpose in mind, scared her to the very bone.

She still believed what some nearly extinct tribal cultures had professed when they first saw cameras: that every photograph taken of you robbed you of a bit of your soul. And these pictures, inside and outside the box, had taken away a large portion of hers. Two small photographs within a tiny homemade coffin within a cardboard box covered with pictures, a Russian nesting doll of her life; the overkill of it made her dizzy. She had to plant her feet more firmly on the porch and even bend her head between her knees—as far as it would go with her arthritis—to keep from fainting. She was glad Alice wasn't there to see that, or she'd have called an ambulance as soon as she was done calling the police.

Was Truman behind it? If he was, what was he trying to get at, to say to her? Why hadn't he just come out and said it over the phone? The little "hand-carved coffin" seemed to be a give-away; it was the name of one of his last books, but anyone could have borrowed that. And the earthworm, and the picture from the graveyard . . . who was responsible for those? Truman wasn't around, and he'd die before he'd touch some creepy-crawly thing.

But then again, the picture from the Clutters' basement; surely he was behind that? Who else would have had it in their possession? Hell, what was he *trying to say?* Or was he trying to say anything? Maybe he was just being strange, sending a reminder from their shared pasts, a signal that he still had a hold over her. But why would he do that? He hadn't spoken to her in nearly twenty years; did she even matter to him anymore? Why get back in touch now? What else was left to say, after the calls of the last few nights? They hadn't been malevolent or threatening; she didn't think he wanted to scare her, but that's the only way she could interpret this box of things from the past and the very near past: it was scary.

And she didn't know why.

You didn't send an aging person a coffin without expecting them to get a little anxious.

Would this be the last chapter of her life, the one her fans had waited on all these years? A last chapter delivered through the mail, that she was then expected to do something with? Maybe she'd known all along that this time would finally come, and that's why she had willed herself to stay alive all these years, when she didn't have much to keep her going but golf and catfish and Alice. Maybe this is what she and Truman had meant, years ago, when they swore they'd always be together.

And as if on cue, as if to confirm she was right, her left index finger began to twitch, the very same finger she had pierced to become blood brothers with Truman. It had happened before; she'd gone to the doctor for it, and he'd told her it was an isolated form of neuropathy, picked up from banging on those stiff typewriter keys all those years. But why it should affect just that one finger, the doctor didn't know.

The finger was tapping and twitching so much she felt like she could leave it alone and let it tap out a telegraph message to Truman, on the armrest of the rocker: dash-dash-dot, nerve synapses shooting straight from her brain to her finger, without going through her heart for processing.

And what the message would spell out, for the recipient on the other end:

What are you doing?

Stop.

What do you want?

Stop.

We've gone this long apart, why come back now?

Stop.

I'll be waiting for your answer.

Stop.

Chapter Six

Truman's feet jerked spasmodically, then quit, tapped out, as he stared blankly at a corner of the room, watching something only he could see, but which he didn't have the energy to respond to or challenge anymore.

The toe tapping had been going on for the last three days, and the sound was about to drive Myrtle out of her mind, if the sight didn't get to her first: her Truman, in bed, in the same baggy boxer shorts and T-shirt he'd been wearing without change, his bare, swollen feet shoved into a pair of tap shoes.

Black tap shoes, at the end of pale, skinny, hairless legs.

Not pretty, not for a minute, no sir, no matter how much she loved him.

Shoes of any kind weren't meant to be worn without socks.

Like she said: who knows what goes on in the minds—and on the feet—of white people?

Myrtle used to think she did.

Suddenly, he started up again. One leg doing a solo number on the bed, the other leg swung off the side and onto the floor. The wooden floor. That's the part that was driving her batty. At least let her put a rug down to muffle the sound.

It didn't take a genius to translate the spasms that were coming from Truman's nervous feet: after the elation of finding the sign from Nancy, he'd gone into a funk, something post-partum after delivering his message on the kites, and nothing could get him out of it, not even his beloved tap dancing.

It used to be the perfect cure-all. Whenever he'd lie in bed for days on end and do nothing but drink and moan, Myrtle could lure him out of his blues with a few well-timed tap steps, or, more to the point, well-tapped time steps.

Now, it was taps for taps, and he wouldn't tell Myrtle why.

Besides, the tapping was her own damn fault. She was the one who'd bought him the shoes years ago, a birthday present for a man who could have bought his own tap shoes a million times over. He said it was the one thing he'd never gotten as a child that he'd always wanted. In an act of desperation—a little child yelling I WANT! I NEED!—he'd even gone as far as nailing bottle caps to his one good pair of church shoes, but that was as close as he ever got to his own pair of taps, until Myrtle answered the call. Nature abhors a vacuum, then fills it, Truman had said, tears in his eyes, when he first saw them. Myrtle said she "abhorred a vacuum" too, not quite getting the poetry of the moment.

The second he slipped them on—this fat, worn-out, middle-aged man—his muscle memory returned: buck and wing, toe-heel-toe, soft shoe, all learned from imitating Saturday-afternoon movies as a child. Myrtle matched him step by step: she'd been a Cotton Club dancer earlier in life—and don't get her started on how she'd gone from that to this—and knew how to shake away the blues, his and hers. (She called hers "the black *and* blues.") The shoes came on, the moves came back, and so did the smile, in Truman's lips and eyes.

That was, until now.

She'd practically shoved the damn things on his feet, but nothing—except for him grunting and rolling over in bed, letting out a big fart as his belly jiggled.

And then, like a fever that broke, he told her why he was depressed: Nancy was still here. Even after sending up the kite, and finding the sign of the dead snake, she wouldn't leave him alone. She was still haunting him. She was there, in the room, right now.

Didn't Myrtle see her?

He couldn't take it anymore.

What did that damn girl want, blood from a stone?

No.

She wanted him to bury the snake.

How could he have done something so inconsiderate—left it out in the hot sun, to bake?

It was like leaving *her* out in the sun, no good to anybody after she was dead.

It hurt her feelings.

Now, Myrtle finally understood why he hadn't said anything for three days: HE HAD LOST HIS MIND, AND EVEN HE KNEW IT.

As if to acknowledge he had a problem, that he was trying to do something about it, and to let Myrtle know he knew, Truman yanked off a tap shoe—the tightness of it leaving a red ring around his pale flesh, even after it was off—and threw it at the wall.

"GO AWAY!"

Then he looked meekly at Myrtle: "It's a start. For now, humor me that she's there, and help me find the snake. It's the only way to get rid of her, once and for all. That, and have Nelle forgive me. It's like making my amends, which as you know was the one part of AA I could never cotton to. Guess that's why they wouldn't have me anymore."

He harrumphed, his own private joke, because he knew as well as Myrtle he'd never even tried to quit. He was lying to himself, as well as the rest of the world.

"You know, ghosts linger on because they still got business to finish. That's Nancy's: bury that snake, then make my peace with Nelle Harper, then she promises she'll move on. AND LEAVE ME THE FUCK ALONE."

Fine.

Just go back, find the snake, wrap its poor blown-off head in gauze, the same way Nancy's head, and all the Clutters', had been wrapped in their coffins, then give it a decent burial.

Truman stood up after he announced his latest brainstorm, dusted off his hands as if to say "And that's that," then executed a tap step that was so furious it knocked him back into bed.

Myrtle knew as well as the next cleaning woman that a snake was never going to look like a person, no matter how much you wrapped up its head, but since this was the only thing that had

gotten Truman out of bed in days, she wasn't about to argue
with him. For now, she went to the medicine cabinet to pull out
the gauze.

Myrtle had finally found out who Nancy Clutter was, but
almost wished she hadn't. She'd kept asking Truman about her, in
the early hours of his funk, as he kept keening her name over and
over; he didn't say a word, just yanked a book out of the bookshelf
by his bed and thrust it at her—after signing it, of course. A mind's
a terrible thing to waste, he said, then started crying and pulled the
covers over his head. She didn't know if he meant her mind or
his. She'd stayed up nights reading the book, keeping her husband up, too, and now she knew something she could never
forget, no matter how much she'd like to. A dead girl with her
head wrapped up, a girl in a coffin, wearing the same red velvet
dress she'd planned to wear to her prom. No wonder Truman was
moody and drunk and haunted most of the time; she'd be, too, if
she had to live with that.

She'd lived through a lot with Mr. Truman, ever since he
bought the house in 1968. She'd liked to tease him by playing
like she didn't know who he was, didn't know that he was on TV
all the time or what he'd written. She saw the books all over the
house, in all the foreign languages and different covers; what they
meant to her was just more to dust. She fixed up the house whenever his big city friends came to visit, but he always told her his
favorite time was just after they'd left, when it was just him and
her again. She'd say, "Mr. Truman, are you flirting with me? You
know my husband won't like that," but he'd just go on about how
she was the only one who really understood him, her and Nelle
Harper, because they reminded him of his childhood, which was
his favorite place to be.

Not the hellhole he was trapped in, here in Palm Springs.

And he didn't mean the weather.

And he didn't mean Myrtle was a bad housekeeper.

He meant something else that he never would explain in words, but Myrtle knew: he wanted to go back home, but couldn't.

That's what it all came down to.

—

By now, days had passed since they'd gone kite flying, and Myrtle wondered if they'd be able to find the snake again. Maybe a vulture or hyena had carted it off. And even if they could find it, what kind of shape would the poor thing be in? Out in that hot sun, decomposing morning noon and night. She knew what a few minutes in the Palm Springs sun did to her, especially the way she'd been feeling lately, worn out and losing weight. Truman was gaining; she was losing; and neither one was trying. No sir, Truman could pick up the snake if he wanted to, but she wasn't about to go traipsing out in the hot sun one more time to touch the damn thing, even if she did say prayers for Nancy Clutter every night now.

Besides, the last thing they needed in the house, even if temporarily, was another snake; Truman already had a menagerie of them. He said they brought him good luck, ever since he'd been bitten by one as a child and survived, at Hatter's Mill Pond. His beautiful white hair had fallen out and his leg had swollen up to the size of an elephant's, but he said it taught him he could survive anything.

Anything but wrapping a damn snake's head up in cheesecloth and pretending it was some girl from Kansas, Myrtle wanted to say.

Only one of the snakes in the house was real; that one was

stuffed and coiled, its mouth open, its fangs bared. Truman had bought it from a local taxidermist. Myrtle was scared to look at the creature, let alone touch its skin, but Truman insisted she keep it oiled up with furniture polish, the kind that was "lemony fresh." She said you don't pay me enough to go touching dead things and you can keep it "lemony fresh" your damn self. Sometimes, he'd bring out a pair of fancy snakeskin boots he owned and hold them next to the real thing: he'd rub the skin on the boots, then the snake, to see if he could detect a difference. He couldn't. That pleased him. It made Myrtle sick.

He had three other snakes, none of them real: one was gold, jointed, and flexible; one of his fancy lady friends had sent it to him years ago, when she was still speaking to him. Truman wrapped it around his flabby arms like a bracelet. He tried to get Myrtle to do it, but she wouldn't, even though she knew it was just a big ol' piece of jewelry. There was also a wooden snake that he'd gotten on a trip to Java, carved out of bamboo and painted with slashes of red and green and blue; his bulldog, Maggie, had a special fondness for that one, and you could practically mark the dog's growth by the size of her teeth marks that fluted up and down the snake's spinal column.

But Truman's pride and joy was yet another one entirely: a white plaster sculpture of a cobra, entwined around a tree limb. Such was the craftsmanship that you could see every separate scale, every piece of rough-hewn bark on the limb. The sculpture hung over Truman's writing desk, so that on those now-rare occasions when he actually made it out of bed to write, it seemed as if the snake was inching down to take a bite out of his head.

It comforted him, knowing the snake was there.

It's what used to drive him to write.

He said he needed a new snake to goad him on now, and he had one—dead and out in the desert, with a bullet hole in its head. If Myrtle wouldn't pick it up, then Mr. Danny would, and if he didn't want to, then there was something else he could pick up: his check on the way out. His services—and there was a broad range of them, only one of which was repairing the AC—would no longer be required at the Palm Springs residence of Mr. Truman Capote and Mrs. Myrtle J. Bennett.

Now, with that settled, they could both break out their tap shoes and celebrate with a dance.

But first, Truman had to get his other shoe back, from the corner where only he could see Nancy Clutter.

Chapter Seven

The police told Alice Lee to go fly a kite.

She told them she'd be happy to, if she survived this latest assault on her sister through the mail, but if she didn't, they were welcome to have her blood on their hands at their next Police Athletic League picnic.

Blood and lemonade; she hoped it mixed.

Good day.

She promptly hung up the phone, and just as promptly returned to the porch to repeat the conversation to her sister. Nelle wasn't surprised; Alice had become the woman who cried wolf, always calling the police with some complaint, imagined or not: someone lingering in front of the house too long; a car slowly driving by; someone asking Nelle, a little too aggressively, for an autograph.

Nelle was glad to have someone ride shotgun for her, but she thought Alice saw things that weren't necessarily there.

This latest package in the mail: just another nut.

Or Truman.

Same thing.

But as Nelle told her sister not to worry and kissed her on the head, Alice Lee saw one more thing for certain: Nelle stuffing something in her pocket that she didn't want Alice to see.

—

But Nelle was worried; this, even more than the dead mockingbird.

Someone spying on her.

Watching.

Waiting.

Was even Truman that crazy, that rattler-nasty?

What if it was someone else? A stranger, following her like that? A stalker? You read about them in the paper all the time . . .

Now she was sounding like Alice.

That was even scarier.

She didn't know how to reach Truman; she didn't have a phone number for him anymore, and hadn't thought to get one when he'd started calling again. She hadn't thought the calls would lead to him terrorizing her, with these pictures from her past, on the inside and outside of a baby coffin. (A coffin just big enough for a baby bird, she just realized. A mockingbird. Was that what he was doing—mocking her? But why? She'd never done unto him; he'd just done unto her.)

It was obvious (wasn't it? now she was doubting herself) that he had sent it; in sending Nelle that hand-carved coffin, Truman might as well have sent his signature in the sky, written with billowy jets of skywriting for all to see. There was no mystery there, except the mystery of why his cat and mouse games, his infuriating cleverness, had slipped so far, why he'd become a riddler whose riddles didn't work anymore.

A hand-carved coffin, indeed. It was the principal device in one of his few recent works that hadn't bombed, and this latest tale had supposedly, *supposedly*, stemmed from their time in Kansas, a tip from one of the detectives.

To a series of seemingly disparate people, all living in the same small town, someone had sent little hand-carved coffins, small enough to hold in the palm of one's hand—a hand no doubt sweaty with fear and confusion once you saw what was inside them: a candid photograph of the recipient, taken unawares. And those seemingly random recipients, one by one, were soon dispatched to their deaths in a singularly gruesome manner: one couple was trapped in a basement fire, their only means of escape barred by a load of bricks; one person had his neck sliced clean through by a razor-sharp, almost invisible wire that had been stretched taut across a side street, to catch him as he drove in his open-air Jeep; another couple had been set upon by rattlers whipped up into a frenzy, waiting in a boiling-hot car with the windows rolled shut.

So much for "Write about what you know."

She thought back to Truman's desperation on the phone, the

confession that he couldn't write anymore: the person to whom you confessed that—as she had confessed in turn to him—wasn't the same person you then turned around to hurt, was it? But then again, regular rules of behavior didn't apply to Truman: he'd dedicated a book to her, then stabbed her in the back. Was this package—her very own hand-carved coffin and all it entailed—supposed to stir up old feelings, or scare her, or get her to do something? She couldn't figure out what. Was she supposed to "read" the pictures on it, and in it, the same way Alvin Dewey had, once upon a time, studied his crime-scene photos looking for evidence? He'd said out loud to them, more than once, "How many animals can I find in these photos?" That's what he called his clues: animals, a rare bit of poetry from a man who was salt of the earth.

That's what she was looking for now—animals.

But whether they were the kind that bit or not, she didn't yet know.

She went up to the attic to find them.

That's where she always went to think, or write, or frankly, escape Alice: a small little lean-to room in the eaves of their one-story house. That's when Alice threw up her hands—a woman rich as her sister, crawling up into a hot, dusty attic to write, like some animal crawling off to die, when she could build a million new offices. But that's what Alice didn't understand, despite their sisterly bond: that Nelle didn't want a big fancy new office. She wanted her past, the cramped spaces in which she had written The Book; she wanted the heat of an attic to sweat the writing out of her. She wanted the walk-up garret she still kept in Manhattan; she wanted the messy corner of her father's law office, upstairs in a forgotten building.

She wanted the past to repeat itself.

That would surprise people: that this woman who claimed to want nothing to do with the past had created a shrine to it, albeit one tucked away inside the drawers of several beat-up file cabinets she had retrieved from her father's law office. (When she went there after he died, and couldn't feel him there anymore, she knew it was time to move on; she packed it all up, even the desk he had used, and hauled it to her house to work—one more tidbit the neighbors used to claim she was becoming Boo Radley, hidden away under the slant of the roof.)

She sometimes played a game with herself: pretending she wasn't the one who had kept all this stuff; she merely kept the stuff her father had kept, all the articles and tributes to and about her, from near the end of his life. That was her excuse: it was *his* tribute, not *hers*, and thus it became her tribute to him; she couldn't get rid of that.

And part of that tribute was the *Life* magazine that had chronicled her, with the pictures that now covered the box in her hands.

That had been her very first thought—that someone had sneaked up into the attic and stolen it, her lone copy of the magazine; she couldn't imagine anybody else holding onto it for all these years. Had that been Truman's doing, too? Just as his phone calls had infiltrated her safe house in the middle of the night, had he hired a thief to do the same, literally? Sneak in and steal the magazine?

It's the only thing that made any sense.

She found herself almost holding her breath as she yanked open the file cabinet drawer, hoping the magazine would be gone.

That, at least, would make sense.

But it was still there.

None of this made sense.

She gingerly lifted the magazine out. From her father having passed it around to neighbors so often—she teased him it was just to show off his own likeness, not hers—the magazine automatically fell open to the pictures of her, taken twenty-five years ago. She looked dark-haired and direct in them, with a smile that hinted at secrets (so unlike others probably saw her today: with a wrinkled face and too-big glasses, her eyes squinting behind them, as if to remember something). Those magazine pictures from so many years ago, nestled next to an ad for All-Bran cereal, which stopped constipation in its tracks.

Had Truman jealously kept a copy of the magazine all these years as well? He'd had more than his share of articles and covers; she'd only ever made the inside. He trumped her when he went back to Kansas to shoot the movie of His Book and made the cover, standing there in black and white on an old dirt road between the two actors who played the killers, a little dwarf sandwiched between the two of them. They didn't know *he* was a killer, in a different way. "Bang bang bang," he'd hold out his fingers and say, shooting his imaginary gun when he didn't like something.

How would Truman like it if she cut up those pictures of him, slapped them on a box, and sent them to him, no note, no P.S., no return address, no nothing except mystery.

What did he *want?*

Damn this brain of hers.

Damn him.

She slammed the drawer shut and threw the magazine across the room.

There.

Think.

She looked at the first photo she'd taken from the tiny coffin she'd just received: let that take her back. Hold it in her hand, close her eyes, and concentrate, just as Truman had taught her to do in the Clutter house.

—

It had not been easy to do, get an audience inside. How they'd pulled that off she really didn't know, even all these years later. All the other reporters had clamored to go, but it was still considered a crime scene, not that they really knew how to process that then; they just didn't want people "trackin' it up." That was as sophisticated as the terminology got. Their entree had been arranged behind the scenes, probably with more than a little help from Marie Dewey. (Oh, how these women pulled the strings. Nelle sometimes thought she and Marie Dewey could have solved the crime on their own, given half a chance. Flashed their smiles, shined their eyes, and gotten a confession from the murderers, if they had just gotten to them first.)

It was her first house of death. Her father hadn't yet died, and although her mother and brother had—within five horrible weeks of each other—their deaths were peaceful, as peaceful as death goes, that is. But these, no—these were violent; ghosts were certain to roam this country farmhouse, looking for release, or revenge. And for all of Truman's grand boasts—the odd characters with whom he'd shared his life journey so far, the part of his childhood he'd spent in New Orleans, full of spells and voodoo— Nelle doubted he'd ever seen the site of four killings any more than she had.

Maybe because of that, he was completely silent for once, struck dumb by the sense of life, and now death, that saturated the place. He walked around on his own, almost reverentially, reaching out to touch things as if trying to divine a spirit from them. He wasn't thinking about writing, not yet. He wanted to know the people first. They weren't allowed to take pictures; they'd have to photograph it with their minds, then compare notes back at the hotel, where Truman bragged he could re-create whole conversations from memory, something he'd been training himself to do since childhood.

Nelle shadowed him at first, the good assistant, then went off on her own. She was a lawyer's daughter; she'd been taught there was a time and place for everything, in terms of talk. She'd also been taught never to commit anything to paper you didn't want getting in someone else's hands. So she knew when to listen: when to listen to other people, and when to listen to the air around her. Truman had taught her that, one of his earliest writing lessons up in their tree house, telling her to close her eyes and smell and listen and feel and see.

"I can't see with my damn eyes closed," she had said, sailor-mouthed at six.

"Yes, you can," he'd said, and indeed, after a few patient moments, she learned she could: close her eyes, and hear the words around her. Now, as adults, she saw Truman do the very same thing: close his eyes and listen to the house, listen to poor Nancy and Kenyon Clutter tell what had happened that night.

After a respectful silence, Alvin spoke up. "This is what we figure happened. The killer comes in—we think it's more than one, with so much blood—the killers come in, don't know if they planned to kill 'em or not, but they get the dad and son and bring 'em down here to the basement . . ."

He stopped, seeing it with his eyes, the same way Nelle and Truman did.

"They never even got to say good-bye to one 'nother, maybe just look in each other's eyes, knowin' what's comin', but . . ."

He became as quiet as Truman, then turned and snapped at him, "So don't you go telling me you don't care about catching the damn killers, Mr. New Yorker."

Truman knew not to answer back; at that moment, he knew he wanted to catch the killers, too.

"That's what gets me the most, those kids, these children—knowing some man was in their house, some monster, knowing that horrors were being done, praying to God to make them stop, but they don't. And then you think maybe God doesn't even . . ."

Exist.

Despite what had happened, what he'd witnessed, Alvin Dewey couldn't say the word; he could barely think it. He would never go that far. "You pray to God you never have to go through something like that in your life."

Nelle had never seen Truman so quiet, so attentive, listening to Alvin Dewey in that cinder block basement.

—

Nelle looked at the picture she held now, of Truman and her there. She squeezed it tight, as if she could squeeze an answer, or at least a few questions, out of it: who was behind the lens, taking the picture, what was special about that moment, compared to any other moment in the house? She knew somebody was taking pictures; others had appeared over the years, just never this one. She remembered that flash of light down in the basement, so bright it made her head snap up in fright at the camera, as if she had just seen the killer herself.

That basement had been tainted by evil, that much was clear, but what was Truman trying to say by sending her a picture of it now, and of them in it? She studied it like Alvin Dewey might have, trying to remember what that good, honest, decent man had taught her: all the clues were there, you just had to stare down the picture until everything else in it disappeared, and you were left with answers.

But she couldn't find them, not yet.

She shifted her eyes to the second picture from the little coffin, shuffling it on top like a card from a deck.

To the uninitiated, it might look like she was weeding any old garden, bent down, yanking at weeds, wearing a sun visor. But if you looked more closely, had special sight, you could see a corner of the little upright slab on which she steadied herself. It was one of three nearly identical markers, a tombstone each for her mother, father, and brother, reminders in chiseled granite and marble of the days when she thought her head and heart would explode with grief and loneliness, after three good-byes too many. Alice seldom went with her to the cemetery anymore; she didn't think it was healthy. As old as she was, she said she preferred spending her company with the living—she'd be spending all her time with the other soon enough.

A picture, taken unawares, in a cemetery; it seemed the most despicable kind of invasion, of intimacy. Had Truman taken it, or hired somebody to follow her there, take her picture and snatch her soul, right out in broad daylight?

Why?

How dare he.

How dare they?

It was enough to drive her crazy, and she ripped both pictures in half.

Good riddance to bad rubbish.

And then she regretted tearing up the pictures, afraid it would bring bad luck, like breaking a mirror. That's what this new intrusion in her life seemed to be: bad luck, or a curse, when she'd done nothing to deserve it.

Somebody wanting a part of her that didn't exist anymore.

She quickly grabbed tape from a dispenser and, one two three, taped the pictures back together.

There.

Now what?

She did what she usually did in that hot, dusty attic.

She took a pad and pen off the desk, then tucked her legs up underneath her in the wooden swivel chair; her joints creaked as much as the old wood did. She'd write a letter to her brother Ed; it's what she always did to calm herself down, just close her eyes and let the pen go. It hardly mattered if she put the pen to paper; the thoughts were always there, paper to land on or not.

She'd been writing the same letter to him, over and over, for years now, asking questions only she could answer. She kept repeating her story, to make sure it had really happened.

It didn't matter that he was dead.

> *My dearest, most precious Ed,*
> *I close my eyes and the first thing that comes to mind is how much I miss you. Not how scared I am right now, or how confused, or how damn mad—even though all those things are true—but how much I miss you. How many times over the years have I written that? Too many. Sometimes I feel your presence, if I pray to God enough before I sit down.*

(I skipped him just now, but hope He'll accept my apology, and let you come through anyway.) I've been feeling your presence a lot lately, always smiling and encouraging me; are you preparing the way for me, Big Brother? Is that what you're trying to say, if I just listen and accept?

Most of me feels like I'm ready to go.

I need you more than ever right now. Somebody has sent me something that has shaken me to my very core. I don't know why it should, I'm so used to getting every kind of crazy thing people send, but this has taken me back to some dark places. You weren't even alive to see the magazine when it came out, nine or ten years after you died, nine or ten years when I lived with a dark cloud of grief over me and in me, and wrote the story of our childhoods as a way out of that grief. (It doesn't seem possible, you being gone so long—I still see you as you were, in your uniform down on the base, holding your two babies. I was such a proud sister and aunt, who wanted to make you proud of me in turn, so I kept you alive in The Book. That's why I gave Scout a brother, not a sister: I still had sisters, but I didn't have you.)

This thing that got left off on the porch, it's covered with pictures from that article, taken when I was in Daddy's old office. I asked them if they wanted me to pretend to write, or really do it. Whichever is more comfortable for you, they said. How could I explain to them that writing was never comfortable for me? I said, Well, let me get going, then you just sneak in, when I'm not looking. (Someone else has just sneaked in, when I wasn't looking.) They sneaked in alright, when I wasn't doing anything except sitting there, frozen, chewing on a pencil to practically keep my teeth from chattering. I had to pick bits of pencil wood out of my teeth after that.

That's what the world thinks a writer writing looks like. (I go into that pose now, to see if it makes things any easier. It doesn't.)

I loved snuggling up in Daddy's old office, tucked up in that corner, like a dog who wants to burrow its way into the darkest, deepest place it can, its butt up to the wall, so nobody can attack it from behind. I think that's what I was worried about—getting attacked from behind. I liked seeing what was out in front of me. After Daddy died, after The Book came out, I'd go to that office all the time, maybe meaning to write, maybe not. Whatever I went there to do, I'd get lost in doing nothing, except getting hypnotized by the dust motes in the air. I thought they held Daddy's very breath, and if I just breathed them in enough, then I could be just like him. I'd take great gulps, then hold them, my cheeks puffed out like the black squirrel that played on the windowsill outside. I'd go through Daddy's desk drawers and pick up objects on his desk and smell them and feel the grease on them and think this came from Daddy's hand or he breathed this same air, so he's still here. I'd go through his cabinets and rearrange stuff, endlessly, then I'd go back and rearrange what I'd already arranged. Sometimes I'd fall asleep, put my head down on his desk and wake up hours later, with a red streak across my forehead, my hair pushed up, and my eyes glued shut.

It wasn't right to grieve that much over one person, but I did, just as I still do, for you.

I can't seem to get away from people dying on me. You must think I'm crazy, going on like this.

Sometimes I think I am.

Daddy's death distracted me for such a long time, then the hullabaloo over The Book; who could write during that, who could even breathe—except stale dust motes in the air? From a book I thought would come out and disappear, to one that did better than a million dreams put together. (But how hard it was: change after change they wanted, and I'd go into their offices and they'd have a new version all marked up, trying to get me to turn it into the book they had in their heads. You can bet there were no dust motes in the fancy offices on Fifth Avenue.) That's tall clover for a country girl like me, who was practically living on Saltines and ketchup soup at the time.

Did they just take it on at first because I was Truman's friend?

I never asked; they never told.

When it began to look like it might turn into something, the questions started up: What are you writing next? How's your next book going? Slow but fine, I'd say, polite Southern girl that I was, and meanwhile I'm hauling Greg Peck around town and meeting Lady Bird Johnson.

Tall clover indeed. Clover for sure, more like hayseed. Truman took that picture of me on the first book jacket, lying in the grass. I'm surprised I wasn't chewing a stalk of it. That was me, dreaming away in the grass—dreaming of other books, dreaming of you? I look back on the last words I ever spoke to the American public and they absolutely haunt me: "I want to be the Jane Austen of south Alabama." I quote, and I quoteth not—it's captured in black and white, you can double-check me. Goodness, why is it that those were practically my last words in print? It's probably good I shut up after that. But did I quit talking, or did they quit asking?

And from dreaming in that grass, to . . . just dreaming, I guess. When did I stop writing, except to you? How do decades go by, and you don't really remember what you did with them? When did the new book I was working on not turn into a book? When did they look at what I had and say no amount of work is going to fix this? All these years later, and I still have the questions, but not the answers.

I didn't need the money, even back then, and that was before every school kid in America had to read It. Riding the bus in Manhattan one time, I saw a little girl up ahead of me reading It. For about two Alabama seconds—although that's a pretty long time, the way we draw things out—I thought about tapping her on the shoulder and saying I wrote that; maybe it'd help her get extra credit or something. But no one would believe her; no one knows what I look like. I'm just some tall, gray-haired lady, who used to be taller, who's spent too much time out in the sun. A tanned but shrinking giant. ("Giants Among Us," that would be a good title for something, but it's probably been used. Most things have; maybe that's why I don't write anymore, there's nothing left to write about.) They'd laugh if they only knew: one of the most famous unseen writers in the world, and I walk among them, and they never even know.

In Monroeville, they know. Last year, for Halloween, I heard giggling out on the porch—children daring each other to come up here for candy, knowing full well who lived here. I opened the door, and they were dressed up like they were in the agricultural pageant at the end of The Book. One of them was a ham, like Scout, encased ramrod straight in chicken wire and paper maché. They thought it was clever—maybe it was an homage, as the snooty French say—but it scared me senseless and I slammed the door.

Alice, of course, tells me it's my own damn fault for opening the door in the first place.

I hate it that I've become Boo Radley.

And now, somebody's managed to not just get me to the door, but to sneak inside the house, with these old, and new, pictures of me. Maybe it's Truman, maybe it's some crazed fan, but whoever it is, I'm scared, and I want to slam the door shut again.

Oh, Brother, how I miss you. Tell me what to do, tell me what they want.

Someday, I'll put all these letters together, present them to the world, and say these are my missing chapters. Do with them what you will, but be kind. I'm going on an old lady now. Maybe I could publish them under a different name, and then, if they like it, say it was me all along, and if they don't, no one's the wiser and I just disappear again.

But I'll never disappear on you.

She never signed the letters. That would be too much of a good-bye. She just folded them up and put them in an envelope, then added them to the full-to-bursting drawer at the bottom of the file cabinet. As she opened the drawer, she held her hands in it, among the other pages on which she had poured out her daily life, and prayed to draw extra strength from them.

They *were* the missing chapters of her life; she didn't know how many more she had left, or how much longer she could keep her secrets hidden, now that there were intruders in the dust, snuck in as stealthily as Dick and Perry had entered that house out in the middle of nowhere, where no one could hear the screams.

Chapter Eight

"NO MORE SNA-A-A-AKES!"

If anybody had been listening to the dry wind that echoed round and round in the Palm Springs desert at that particular moment, that's the scream they would have heard, as Danny pushed out the last syllable and spit into the sand.

"No more snakes, that's right, that's telling 'em!" he thought to himself.

He added a final exclamation point by grinding the spit into the sand with the toe of his boot, but whether by "'em" he meant them—the snakes—or him—Truman—he wasn't even sure himself. Maybe a little bit of both, the snakes and Truman: "same fuckin' thing" he mumbled, part of the ongoing conversation he'd been having with himself for the past two hours, ever since Truman had delivered his ultimatum: get the snake, or get packing. Truman had delivered another ultimatum, almost to himself: a snake with a bullet in it, or a bullet hole in his own head; he said it was one or the other, and he'd been acting so squirrelly lately, Danny didn't doubt him.

But even in the vast, empty desert, with no one to see or hear him, Danny was almost afraid to curse the little man—the little man who now had him hauling up a dead rattler, if he could find it first.

"NO MORE!"

He yelled it into the open sky, a "take that" he was rehearsing for Truman in person.

Pouring the dregs of his beer into an S shape in the sand, he watched the foam bubble up and fry away in the desert heat. He kicked at this lump of sand rather than grind it up, but his words had none of the same kick in them; they were more of a defeated whisper:

"No more snakes."

He might as well have been saying "No more life."

This life.

His life, that had twisted and turned from lucking into a cash cow like Truman to hauling up dead rattlers for him.

Some luck.

Danny had seen and smelled a dead snake only once before: a family had kept one as a pet, and it had crawled into their central air system and died. For days before it was found, the air kept getting warmer and warmer, no matter how low they turned down the thermostat, and smellier and smellier, until finally Danny was called. He retched when he walked into the house, retched even more when he pulled the snake—what was left of it—out of its final resting place.

He swore that was the last time he'd have anything to do with snakes.

But that was before he'd met Truman, one night when he flew into the tiny Palm Springs airport, where Danny moonlighted as a grease monkey, gassing up the planes. Nozzle in hand, Danny filled up tanks while he dreamed and schemed about the fat-cat man or woman, didn't matter which, who'd offer to take him away from it all. He could roll up his shirtsleeves so they bunched up his biceps and made him look fit; unbutton his shirt to there so it showed off a nice little thatch of hair—didn't matter that it was just about the only hair on his head or chest, it looked good on top of the V-shaped tan he managed to get working outdoors most of the time. If you looked hard, you could still see the X-ray of the man he used to be, before a wife and kids and humping two dead-end jobs took over. And make no mistake: pumping gas was a dead end: always smelling like diesel, the vapors going to your head and making you sick, scrubbing your skin so hard every night it rubbed off raw and red, the wife always yelling you smelled up the house, made it stink like it was about to blow up if somebody struck a match.

The man he used to be: that must have been what caught Truman's eye the first time they saw each other, as Truman walked down the stairs from his plane and across the tarmac. Danny knew he had the hook halfway in when Truman gave him a wink, and in return, Danny gave him his card: who knew when his air conditioner might break down? Lucky thing it did, or at least that's what

Truman said. That time, at Truman's house, Danny got a bigger wink, and a pinch on the butt. (And if his butt was bigger and fleshier than it had been a few years ago, well, some guys liked that. More to hang on to.) Danny saw the books with Truman's name on them, the checks Truman left lying around, the stack of pages from the new book he was working on. There were a lot of pages; there would be a lot of checks coming in from that haul.

That's when Danny decided: it was gonna take a lot of time to get Truman's AC up and running to where it should be. Even if Danny had to break a few extra things first, to come back and fix them later. And so what if Danny's wife was threatening to leave him if he didn't spend more time at home. Where was he all the time? Why wasn't he at home for dinner anymore with the kids? Why didn't he want to have sex with her anymore?

That was then, this was now: now, Truman's AC was running just fine, but Danny was out in the vast middle of the desert, looking for a snake with a shotgun blast to its head.

Where was his AC, while he was out here, hot and boiling in the desert?

He'd thought about finding any old snake and shooting it in the head himself. A dead snake was a dead snake was a dead snake, period, right? Wrong. Truman, almost reading his mind, had said, "Don't bother coming back unless you come back with the right one. And I'll know which one that is. I never forget a snake."

Danny felt like that snake, racing away on its belly, knowing a man was standing behind, holding a shotgun to his head.

In Danny's case, that man was Truman.

Danny had been in control at first; somewhere, somehow, the tables had turned, and Truman was on top now, in more ways than one.

"NO MORE SNAKES!"

That felt good, to yell, get it out of his system.

Nobody could stop him from yelling out here as much as he wanted.

Nobody was around to hear.

The sun was at two o'clock—not directly overhead, but the perfect angle to hit under the brim of Danny's Peterbilt cap and blind him, and leave a beet red burn across his jaw. He'd had a lot of time to think as the sun migrated from high noon to two o'clock; think about the unfairness of his life, and think up what to do about it. Truman said he just needed some guidance; now, he had to prove how smart he really was. Hooking up with Truman was the first smart thing Danny had ever done; he had to do something else that was smart now, and not get stuck hauling rattlers for the rest of their "relationship."

That's what Truman called it.

Danny called it a "business opportunity," but he had to come up with something new, and fast, before it turned into a "going out of business sale."

By the time Danny finally found the damn snake—what was it now, three days after he'd originally stumbled over it?—all the moisture had soaked out, and ants and flies had eaten away everything that wasn't nailed down. All that was left was skeleton and cartilage and papery skin.

Three days, but no Resurrection for this lowly creature.

Taking another long chug of beer for courage, and putting on an old pair of work gloves, Danny scooped up the remains and laid them on top of an old gunnysack, the four corners of which he carefully crisscrossed and tied together.

And for just a second, he burst into tears: they came rushing out of him, but he squeezed them back as fast as they came. DAMNITWASN'TFAIR. Working so hard, just minding your own Goddamn business, not getting any breaks, not hurting anybody, then getting whacked out in the desert and left to rot: whether he was recounting the litany of his own life's sorrows, or the snake's, he didn't know.

And he didn't care.

FUCKIT.

That was all about to change.

Just screwing Truman wasn't enough.

Helping him make Goddamn kites.

Putting up with that busybody housekeeper.

Doing the SHITWORK while Truman bitched and moaned and rolled around in his bathrobe saying he was working.

Danny would show him what real work was.

He wiped his forehead with his sleeve, mopping up sweat and tears with one fell swoop.

He wasn't going to cry anymore.

He *was* smart: he'd just come up with a plan.

Chapter Nine

.

How many minutes out of her life had Nelle spent in front of coffins and dead people?

Too many to count.

How many had she imagined?

Even more.

And now she was making yet another return trip, to the cemetery where her brother Ed was buried. She was always in the mood for a visit after writing him one of her letters, but knew that a trip to the boneyard every time would set even more tongues wagging than already wagged: a woman who barely left her own house except to see the resting place of dead people. (And those were just the trips she made on foot; if they only knew how often she traveled there in her mind.) No, an outing to the cemetery wasn't always a good idea for her, let alone the gossipy neighbors, but now she had work to do: Truman, or somebody, seemed to be directing her there. That's the only thing she could think of to do, spurred on by the picture of herself, standing graveside. It had been the scene of one of their earliest life (and death) lessons; now, was there something else to be learned there?

And it wasn't just Truman who seemed to be pointing the way there; Brother was, as well. Usually when she wrote him—oh, neighbors, get a load of this! The crazy lady authoress writing letters to her dead brother!—she felt as if he were communicating right back. But with this last letter, there had been no answers from the other side, just the echo of her own questions. No, if she wanted to talk to Brother today, she'd have to meet him halfway, in his current place of residence: the cemetery. It seemed as logical a place as any to start looking.

But start looking for what?

—

The ground was damp; you'd think after all these years she would have learned her lesson and worn sturdier shoes after a rain shower. Step, sink, step, sink. She'd have to leave these in the mudroom, even though that's what it was for, and Alice would kick up a fuss about having to take one of her good steak knives to whittle off the dried mud. But Nelle had rushed out of the house with no thought to footwear, let alone her sister's good steak knives: she'd just thought of a taped-up photograph, taken in a graveyard, that seemed to be directing her right back there. She didn't want to take the picture with her, stick it in the bottom of her purse along with her mints and Kleenex and cigarettes. She didn't want it contaminating anything else it might touch, but she couldn't forget it, either.

She'd never forget it.

Nelle's friend Tom Butts brought her to the cemetery; he was often her traveling companion on such journeys. He'd recently retired from preaching, and now saved his sermons for her and the catfish they competed over catching. Tom served two roles these days, chauffeur and spiritual advisor; Nelle wasn't sure which one she needed more right now, when she was too shaken to drive. Tom always knew when she wanted conversation and chatter; he also knew when to offer silence and let her wander alone, while he went off to do rubbings of the tombstone epigraphs he hoped to collect in a book someday.

Now, Tom knew something was wrong.

"I know *who* we're gonna find here, same old dead people we always do, but who, or what, are you *looking* for? Your eyes haven't stopped dartin' around since we pulled through the gate. You havin' a fear of ghosts all the sudden?"

No, just the person who seemed to have trained a bead on her head, and shot her—with a camera. That person who might be aiming to shoot her again, now. That person who seemed to know what she was up to before she did. That person who wanted to draw her into the clearing of a cemetery, for . . . whatever.

Maybe somebody who was *really* pissed off that she'd never written a sequel to The Book.

"Olly, olly, oxen free," Nelle suddenly yelled out.

"What the heck was that about?" Tom asked.

"Just had to get it out of my system," she answered.

But of course, no one answered her back, not even an echo.

She was suddenly as pissed off as the person awaiting a sequel that was never going to come: she was pissed off that she was becoming a scaredy-cat. She never used to be afraid of anything, but lately, even before she got the package, she'd felt her nerve fading up and shrinking, just like her body. She didn't know if it was old age she was afraid of, mad at, or somebody sending strange packages, but her "Olly, olly oxen" cry was a warning: she was pissed.

And scared.

On this, holy ground.

There were plenty of places for someone to hide: behind the trees that bordered the grounds, in the shadows of the tall mausoleums that belonged to some of Monroeville's finest families, underneath the Spanish moss that cascaded from the trees like widow's weeds. She used to put it in her hair like a wig when she was little, until Truman told her it was infested with chiggers and she'd have to have her scalp scrubbed raw with kerosene—and, he added, set on fire—to get rid of them. She trusted the chiggers part; the kerosene part sounded like something Truman had cooked up on the spot. She didn't drape the hanging, airborne plant in her hair anymore, although all these years later, she still couldn't help but marvel at it; the South wouldn't be the South without it.

This cemetery wouldn't have hiding places without it.

She wouldn't be scared without it.

"Somethin' happen?" Tom asked again. "You know you can tell me most anything."

But she couldn't tell him this. Whatever this was, or was to become, she knew it was hers alone, and not to be shared.

"Just feelin' guilty 'cause I've been neglectin' the graves. Let's get on with it."

They continued walking, Nelle on the lookout, Tom on the lookout at her, their shoes sucking at the mud. He'd buried half the people in here, and knew the secrets they'd taken with them to their graves. Even though he wasn't a Catholic priest, he'd been their father confessor. He wanted to tell Nelle it wasn't too late for her to tell him her secrets, especially the secret of what was scaring her so much on this hallowed ground, but he couldn't find the words.

Neither could she.

Words: they were the things both of them knew best, and now neither one of them could find the right ones.

—

Nelle's first trip to the cemetery had come long before her family started being buried there, when six-year-old Truman dragged her there by the hand. It was to the funeral of the man who'd been pulled out of Hatter's Mill Pond after drowning and being chomped on by water snakes. (The "chomped on" part—that was something else Truman had dreamed up.) The dead man had been a worker at the mill; his demise was said to be an accident, although Truman and Nelle, having read one too many police gazettes at the barbershop, never saw anything as a straightforward accident. It was so much more exciting to imagine everything was a murder, or a conspiracy.

They used the word without knowing what it meant.

They didn't know the "Snake Man," as they'd taken to calling him; his burial was just something to do, a way to pass a hot

Saturday afternoon when there weren't enough nickels for the movies. It would be Nelle's first funeral, something her parents would have skinned her alive for doing if they'd ever found out. She almost got caught when she conceded to the solemnity of the occasion by wearing a clean T-shirt under her overalls; that set off so many suspicions she almost spilled the beans. Truman wore a starched, all-white linen outfit; nobody was suspicious of him because that's what he always wore.

By the time they got to the ceremony, the minister was in full swing, his oration having taken him just inside the Pearly Gates but not yet to the feet of the Heavenly Throne. Truman and Nelle were forced to stand at the back of the crowd that was gathered around the coffin, but they wouldn't stay there for long: Truman was desperate to see what the Snake Man looked like, and what the mortician—another one of his newfound favorite words—had done to reduce the swelling Truman imagined had overtaken the body, and hopefully the face.

"I want to see his eyes; see if they froze up looking into the Jaws of Death, or if they're just puffy from all the venom. I know I can tell the difference."

". . . and just how you gonna do that? They'll know we're not kin."

Indeed. The Snake Man was black, and the assembled mourners were shunted off to a small, enclosed parcel of the cemetery just for colored people.

This time, Truman and Nelle were even more of a minority than they usually were.

Of course, Truman already had the whole thing planned out.

"There's a part at the end where everybody files past the coffin to pay their last respects, before they cover it up. Just follow the crowd; everybody'll be wailing away so much they won't notice two more bodies, even if they are lily white like us."

They waited for the final lines of "The Old Rugged Cross" to be sung, then made their way up front. The victim's face and eyes were indeed puffy; it hadn't been just Truman's runaway imagination. Snake Man was even a little bit green, underneath the already dark skin, or maybe that was Nelle's runaway imagination, looking at her first dead body.

Truman immediately began ruminating on how it must have felt: that first puncture bite from the snake's fangs, the chomp the old mill hand must have felt at the same time he was gulping water, trying to bat the snake away and swallowing even more water, and thrashing, and even after he went unconscious, what it was like in his cells and skin as they absorbed water and began expanding like sponges . . .

(And they wondered how Truman could have written something like In Cold Blood. Nelle laughed to herself, thinking back to that first funeral. He'd been writing it since he was six years old.)

The singing over, the crying in its last throes, people soon began drifting away, but Truman wanted to see the ritual through to the bitter end: the coffin lowered into the open grave, the dirt shoveled on top. He and Nelle waited until everyone was gone, even the family, and the field hands had started dumping in the dark, loamy earth on top of the plain wooden coffin. What a dead, dull sound it made, like heavy, muddy raindrops about to burst; Truman scooped up a handful and tossed it in himself, closing his eyes so he could remember how to describe the sound later, in the little reporter's pad he always carried with him.

"Swear on it," he said, in a passion, to Nelle. "Swear you'll never tell another soul about our being here, our very first funeral. I want it to be just ours, forever and ever . . ."

"I swear." Somehow, even at that young age, Nelle understood the importance of keeping promises.

They touched together the fingers that had already shed blood. Their pact was done, but Nelle wasn't.

"What if he wakes up inside, and starts scratchin' on the lid of the coffin to get out?"

"That's impossible. They drained all his blood out and pumped him full of something that would kill him outright, even if he wasn't already dead."

"I hope they do that to me."

"They do it to everybody."

"I don't wanna wake up in no coffin, tryin' to scratch my way out. I'd rather scratch my eyeballs out, so I couldn't see how dark and scary it was."

Then and there, Nelle decided she wanted no part of being put in a coffin and buried in the ground; she wanted to be set on fire and turned into glistening white ash, to be scattered all over town. She wanted everything about her to be returned to the earth, and the ashes of every page she'd ever write incinerated as well, indistinguishable from her very remains. Her letters to Brother, the books the world never saw. All of her, scattered to the four winds, instead of trapped in a prison of pink-lined satin.

It would feel good to be set so free.

—

Almost undone by the sensation of memory, of flight, of being transformed into a hundred million snowflakes of bone and ash,

Nelle lost her balance and reached out to the Snake Man's tombstone to keep from falling.

Tom rushed over. "You still taking that vertigo medicine?" he said, as he took her free arm and guided her to sit on top of the tall stone.

"I'm fine. P.S. Just remind Alice I wanna be cremated, no matter what kind of fuss she makes."

Tom watched as she closed her eyes and rubbed the Snake Man's marker, the marble so worn over by verdant green moss it was almost hidden from view. She always sought out the grave and offered a prayer of contrition whenever she was there. All these years later, she was still making up for that first petty crime, of being an interloper at a stranger's funeral. Now, she knew how sacred funerals were, having attended so many; they weren't to be taken lightly.

She opened her eyes and made a quick sweep over the area, looking for—she still didn't know what. It wasn't easy being a detective with a man of the cloth looking on, but she couldn't let Tom know what she was up to. She had to find whatever she was looking for on her own, and with that in mind, she patted the Snake Man good-bye and moved on to her own family plot.

She could find it blindfolded, and with every sense gone: take away her sight, she'd smell her way there. Take away sight and smell, she'd listen to the particular whistle of the wind as it zigzagged through the tombstones and find the right place. Take away her ability to hear and taste and smell, and even walk, and she'd be able to crawl her way there, bearing gifts of remembrance: a jelly jar filled with wildflowers, a piece of candy or caramel cake, even a simple, polished stone she'd pick up on her way there. It wasn't insanity, to her mind, but pure Southern manners: you never went empty-handed when you went calling. Today, she'd brought the letter she had just written to Ed; she'd put it on top of the marker for a while, let it soak up his presence, then take it back, to her own file cabinet burial plot at home.

Maybe she'd take more of him back with it.

Nelle and Tom arrived in front of the row of three: Mother, Brother, Father, in that order. There were spaces next to them for the other sisters, but Nelle would be declining that invitation, thank you very much. Let them scatter her ashes over the golf course. They kept begging for an invitational named in her honor; her ashes would be as close as they got.

Tom stood next to her, his fingers intertwined with hers for an appropriate interval of silent prayer, then he walked away, allowing Nelle her privacy—although not before he saw her glance nervously around yet again. Even as he wandered off, looking for inspiration for a new sermon in God's natural wonders, he kept a watchful eye on his old friend, who in turn kept a watchful, nervous eye on everything around her.

If somebody was going to shoot her, with a gun or a camera, there was little she could do about it. She'd made the decision on her own to come to this place; now, she'd let go and let the place take her wherever it wanted to. Inevitably, it was back to the darkest time of her life, when she buried her family one by one.

—

Her mother played piano and organ at the local church, so it was strange not to hear her playing one of them at her very own funeral. (Of course she couldn't; she was dead. It took Nelle a beat to remember that.) Some other woman, someone Nelle didn't know, was doing it, pumping out "The Old Rugged Cross" yet again.

It was a very popular song.

Nelle was twenty-five, but it was only the second funeral she had ever attended, after the Snake Man's.

Her mother lay in a rosewood coffin lined with pink satin, her white powdered skin and hair glowing almost red-orange from all the lights focused on her. The air seemed to get warmer the closer Nelle got to the coffin; when she finally reached it, she stared at the face, praying for the lips to move, or the eyes to twitch, one last time.

Five impossible weeks later, Nelle would be asked to repeat the same procession, step by step, this time to bury her brother. He had died suddenly of a brain aneurysm when he was just thirty, and Nelle five years younger.

Coming back, to plan the funeral of the one who had planned the funeral.

It was unimaginable.

Inside that viewing room, the very same place her mother had lain, Nelle had to work her courage up slowly, in increments, before she could look at him. Moving flower arrangement by arrangement, and there were many, for her brother had been very beloved, she got nearer and nearer the coffin, all the while wondering if his brain had hurt when it exploded. Still not able to take in the coffin, she instead took in the elements of the formal mourning room, to calm herself. Breathing slowly, forcing herself to breathe at all, she studied the walls, then the artwork on them, then the damask-covered couches and chairs, and only after she had completed a thorough inspection of those did she even allow her gaze to move to the closed lower half of Ed's coffin, and only then to her brother's body inside: his hands resting by his sides, his stomach, his torso, his neck, and then, finally, his face.

How still, how completely unlike her brother it was, no trace remaining of anything that had once been alive. The difference between that, and this . . . nothing—a body that looked as if it had never moved in the world at all, never played with her as a child, never had children himself—was staggering.

This body was so dead it didn't even know its soul was missing.

On an impulse—something to do with her hands, to keep them from tearing out her hair and shoving handfuls of it at Heaven in fury—Nelle put her hands in the pocket of her suit jacket and found a dusty peppermint that had come out of its wrapping. (Where had that come from? Probably her mother's funeral, just five weeks earlier. It was the last time Nelle had worn the suit.) She put that lonely peppermint in the coffin, next to her brother; it had been their favorite candy as children, and it would sustain him on his next journey.

It was all she could do not to crawl into the coffin herself.

"Flights of angels, sing thee to thy rest."

Those were her final words to him.

She'd never known what they meant until then.

—

Mother, Father, Brother.

Three graves, three unbearable sets of memories, one set of plastic flowers, in front of Ed's tombstone.

Who put those there?

Not her, not Alice.

Having nothing at all there was better than plastic flowers.

Nelle bent down to pull them out, the same pose she had been in when that last picture was taken, and pulled up clumps of mud along with the plastic stems. They came realistically complete with their own molded thorns.

She jerked her hand away, pricked.

But it wasn't just the thorns: it was another box, hidden behind the plastic flowers, just like the one that had been left on her porch, wrapped in the same blank brown paper.

She couldn't have been any more shaken if Ed's very arm had shot up through the earth and grabbed her by the throat.

She grabbed at the package like a dog at a bone, a bone with meat on it, and ripped the paper off. Underneath was another cardboard shell, this one covered with a different assortment of pictures, all in miniature: blades of grass, a tree in the distance, a horse rearing up, and one long, rectangular tombstone of granite with four mounds of earth in front of it.

Something flickered in her brain—her racing, skyrocketing brain—but she didn't stop to think what it was before she pulled open the top.

Inside, as before, a tiny, hand-carved coffin.

She didn't even take the time to look inside, for what other pictures might be awaiting her, but struggled to get up and yell to Tom that they had to go.

"Now."

These were the graves of people she loved.

Somebody had transgressed here.

Somebody had transgressed *them*.

"Get me outta here. Quick."

As Nelle tried to hide the sin in her purse, Tom came rushing.

"Dear precious Lord, what in the heavens is wrong? You don't look at all well. I turn my back for a second, and . . ."

"Just take me home. Please. I can't stay here. I don't know if I can ever come back here again."

She hated whoever had made her feel that way.

—

Alice had to hurry, while her sister was digging up graves.

On the front porch, Alice had seen her sister hide something behind her back, something else that had come in that package from Hell. This was too small a house for secrets, secrets between two sisters. There had been far too many secrets for the last umpteen years.

Alice Lee didn't miss anything; she deserved her own book for everything she had witnessed.

"Old Women and Their Tennis Shoes," that would be a good title for the autobiography of Alice, the great author's sister.

No, "Old Women in Their Tennis Shoes, Who Sneak Around Where They Shouldn't," that would be an even better title—a more honest title—because that's exactly what Alice was doing right now, sneaking around in her sister's attic lair, the moment she was gone. Alice, who as a lawyer had sworn on more oaths and documents than anyone standing, had just broken the ultimate oath she'd made to her sister years ago, by violating the private space she said she'd never enter.

And it wasn't her first time.

She could pretend she was searching for some long-lost document, or Christmas ornaments that had been stuck up in the attic (even though Christmas was months away). Alice, who could rationalize anything with her lawyer's mind, could even persuade herself she was there for her sister's safety, and her own: if some crazy person was running around sending them even crazier things, then Alice had a right to know, and protect them accordingly. She wanted to know if she was about to be murdered in her sleep, or if somebody was going to send *her* a coffin with her name on it. But she wouldn't take it, she would tell you that right now. She'd march it right back to the post office—after giving the postman who'd delivered it a tongue lashing—and say, "You can ship this right on back to wherever it came from, and I shudder to think where, because I am not at home now or ever to receive any such thing."

Oh, yes, Alice Lee could play like she was protecting her family and looking at tiny coffins that had come unsolicited in the mail, but she knew the real reason she was here: to see what her sister had been up to for the last twenty-five years.

Was there another book up here or not?

She was as curious as the rest of the world, hand-carved coffin be damned.

Even she didn't know what her sister got up to when she came up here, and they lived under the same roof. Alice would hear the peck peck peck of the same typewriter Nelle had had all these years and wonder, was that the new book, or just the same old answers to the same old fan letters? Had she ever written another one, after the first? She'd told plenty of people she was working on one, and even had an idea for a third one.

Were they all lies?

No.

It wasn't her business what her sister did—or didn't do.

She was ashamed of herself for even thinking such a thing.

Get on with what she had come for: what had Nelle Harper hidden behind her back, down there on the porch?

The little coffin, now resting on Nelle's desk.

She picked it up, then immediately dropped it, thinking what if the police wanted to fingerprint it, and found her fingerprints on it, then hauled her off. (She didn't watch TV, but she heard the stories; she knew anything was possible.)

But from underneath the coffin, she'd seen it, what she guessed Nelle Harper had hidden from her: two photographs, torn in half and then Scotch-taped back together. She picked them up, too curious to remember the issue of fingerprints: had they come in the mail torn up like that? She knew what they were, at least what the pictures were of: her sister Nelle, down in Kansas with that Truman, and Nelle out at the graves.

But why?

In that, she and her sister were exactly the same. They knew what they were, but not why.

Alice started moving things around on the desk, looking for answers. Then she began looking beyond the things on the desk; she found herself opening drawers and cabinets that were covered with dust, sneezing with the dust mites. How did her sister *work* up here? And hiding behind that question, another one: what did she *do* up here? That was the real question, even if she swore the opposite up and down to a dozen people who asked every day.

Damn it! She couldn't keep her mind from going back there, even when she'd just held a little coffin in her hand.

She got so mad at herself that she slammed a drawer on her finger. And she started crying, not because of the pain, but for doubting her sister, and even worse, the scariest thought of all, the one that hovered just at the bottom and edges of her consciousness, after all these years: had Truman helped her with The Book?

Is that why Nelle had never written anything else?

Damn that coffin and that other box that had come into their house and poisoned her mind with such thoughts (thoughts that had been there long before any such package arrived).

When she found herself wrapping her blouse around her hands (no fingerprints!) before she opened even more drawers, she knew in her heart she was committing the worst of sins—not that the police would ever know, but her sister would, and that was the greatest sin of all, doubting her sister after all these years.

She couldn't get out of that room fast enough.

How many minutes of her life had Alice spent wondering these things about her sister?

Too many to count.

Chapter Ten

It was too late at night to hire a hit man, so Truman got a box of sugar to do the job instead.

Why?

To pour in Mr. Danny's gas tank. And that wasn't lovey-dovey talk for anything else: Truman said his gas tank, he meant his gas tank. On his car. Nowhere else. Truman had read somewhere that sugar in a tank would keep a car from running, now he'd find out. It was the nastiest thing he could think to do on short notice, after what Mr. Danny had done to him: come back from the desert rip-roaring drunk and lassoing an old gunnysack over his head.

Myrtle could smell him before she saw him, as he tore into the house.

"I'm better 'an this, haulin' up rattlers and scorchin' my ass off, and he's gonna know that for once. I've got a plan. Everybody thinks I'm just a dumb fuck, well, I've been lookin', I've been listenin' . . ."

Before Myrtle could stop him, he used the sack to bang open the door to Truman's inner sanctum, the room no one was ever supposed to go into—except Myrtle, armed with Spic and Span—and saw a million pairs of eyes staring back at him. Truman's eyes, in psychedelic colors. The four walls, and even the ceiling, were plastered with the Warhol print of Truman that had been on the cover of *Interview* magazine. Guess Mr. Andy with his Polish last name and silver white wig didn't know it could be wallpaper, too. (Myrtle did; she was the one who'd been flat on her back for days, pasting the covers onto the ceiling, the Michelangelo of the Palms.)

Even Mr. Danny, pumped up with booze and piss and sun and resentment, stopped short at the sight of all those eyes in all those colors.

"STOP STARING AT ME! I CAN'T TAKE IT ANYMORE! No more STARING! And no more SNAKES!"

He threw the sack at the wall and the remains came flying out. Myrtle thought she'd never see a flying snake as long as she lived; now she could scratch that one off the list, just as she saw it land on Truman.

"You wanted that Goddamn snake. There. Have at it. Bury it. Fuck it for all I care, 'cause you sure ain't fuckin' me no more. It's yours. I've got a *plan*."

He grabbed a stack of foolscap pages that were stacked neatly beside Truman's typewriter—albeit a little splattered now, by decomposing snake—and said what he'd been rehearsing in the hot sun all afternoon:

"Seems like a pretty fair trade to me. You got what you want: a snake. I got what I want: your book. After I read it, I'll figure out what it's worth, and may the highest bidder win. Your precious baby is now officially being held ransom. Teach you to treat me like dirt out in the sun . . ."

It was the book Truman had worked on for the last decade of his life, his masterwork.

When Truman wasn't making snake boxes or flying kites or drinking, he talked about it. He talked about it a hell of a lot more than he actually wrote it: his exposé of the high-society ladies of New York, his former best friends, his swans. He'd already published a few chapters from it in Esquire magazine, spilling their secrets—the glamour girls who had started out as hookers, or their rich and powerful and silver-haired husbands who fucked the maids while the wives were gone. No one had ever written anything like that before. Truman might as well have used real names. He'd been run out of town on a rail, abandoned by his swans, when he'd thought they'd just all get a good laugh out of it.

The joke was on him.

Now, he was close to finishing it.

He'd been close to finishing it for years.

The masterwork no one had ever seen, that would top even In Cold Blood.

It was years overdue at the publishing house.

And this was the only copy in existence.

In Danny's snake-stained hands.

Truman grabbed his chest as if he were having a heart attack and opened his mouth to scream, but the words froze.

And if a flying snake was rare, the sight—and silence—of a speechless Truman was even more rare. In fact, it was unknown, and lasted for just that split second.

If he was a good writer, he was an even better yeller: with a gun to her head, Myrtle couldn't have described the sound that came out of his mouth, and soul. Later, she would swear she had seen Truman's tongue fork in two, darting in and out of his mouth and licking at his lips. She would swear she had seen him become one of his snakes.

His eyes narrowed to little slits and he hissed as Danny high-tailed it out of the house, flicking little bits of serpent flesh off his shoulders.

As he ran past her, Myrtle was hit by a hot flash, but it had nothing to do with the change of life or the excitement of the past few minutes or even the heat radiating off Danny's body.

No, it was hot as the blazes in there. *Shit.* The AC had just gone out again. Now who the Sam Jackson were they gonna get to fix it?

Truman's scream pierced the heat and took her mind off Yellow Pages and repair calls.

"That man is *dead*. DEAD! My life! He's taken my LIFE! Now he's gonna PAY WITH HIS . . ."

—

Myrtle didn't get how a box of sugar—and confectioners' sugar, at that; it was the best she could do on short notice—in Mr. Danny's gas tank was gonna make him pay with his life, but that's how she and Truman came to be sitting across the street from his house, waiting for his lights to go out.

I'll punch his lights out, Truman thought.

Oh my God, why hast Thou forsaken me, Myrtle thought.

She'd been counting on that box of sugar to make a coconut cake; that was before Truman had grabbed it out of her cupboard without even asking, and pulled her along with it. (Damn if people weren't snatching up things left and right tonight. If it wasn't nailed down, you could bet good money somebody would take it.) And how Truman loved her coconut cake—and that wasn't lovey-dovey talk for anything else, either. She said coconut cake, she meant coconut cake. With icing. On a plate. Nowhere else.

Sometimes a thing was what you called it; sometimes it wasn't.

Sometimes her Truman went insane; sometimes he didn't.

Tonight, he'd gone insane, aided and abetted by a bottle of J&B Scotch and Nancy's snake, splattered all over his inner sanctum.

Truman and Myrtle were crouching in hiding behind a row of bushes when Truman announced that Myrtle was going to be the one to race across the street and pour in the sugar.

He called her his "Wilma Rudolph."

She called him her "road to ruination."

"Why am I the one runnin' my way into a life of crime, 'stead of the other way around? Seems YOU'RE the one met his sorry ass in the first place. Seems YOU'RE the one has a book sittin' in that nasty low-rent house of his, 'cause if it was MY book, wouldn't be sittin' in nobody's house, but flyin' off the shelves. Bestseller for sure, after I write up everything you put me through . . ."

"If you ever go tellin' my tales outta school, it's gonna be a hell of a lot more than sugar I'll pour down your gullet . . ."

"Forget the sugar, you still haven't told me how him not being able to run his car's gonna help you get your big ol' book back . . ."

"One thing at a time. First we gotta scare him . . ."

"I know some people scared a' packin' on a few pounds, but how in God's green earth some sugar's gonna scare him . . ."

Their back-and-forth tirade was interrupted when Mr. Danny's house finally went dark.

"There. Now's your chance, Wilma."

"At least nobody's gonna spot me. There's no moon out."

Truman pushed Myrtle up; she looked like a mastodon trying to lumber her way out of extinction and the La Brea Tar Pits at the same time. She looked left and right, for safety's sake, then darted—as fast as a mastodon could dart—into the shadows across the street. As she moved, she rubbed the box of confectioners' sugar like a rosary: "Jesus God, protect my black ass, and forgive the sins I commit in the name of that little white pipsqueak I work for."

It was then she discovered a kink in the plan. That box of sugar had been sitting in the cupboard for weeks, if not months. Inside the cardboard, the granules had lumped together like a square brick. That sugar wasn't going in anybody's tank. Only thing you could do with it was brain somebody in the head, which is exactly what she felt like doing to Truman.

She turned back around and hissed at him, "This ain't gonna work."

Truman hauled himself up and joined his partner in crime in the middle of the street.

At 2 A.M.

A streetlamp cast their two shadows over the neighborhood.

From inside his bedroom, Danny couldn't help but see what looked like shadow puppets—one tiny, the other enormous—on his wall. (His wife and children were so fed up with him they had moved out to her mother's; for now, he was all alone in the house.) He staggered out of bed—the booze headache was really beginning to lock in on his brain—and raised the window a crack to listen to their voices drift up through the night:

"What the hell you mean it's not gonna work?"

"See for yourself . . ."

Truman felt the heft of the sugar brick in his palm.

"I don't pay you good money to keep old food in the house, goin' bad on us . . ."

"How the hell I know you were gonna be usin' it for a lethal weapon?"

"Way you cook's lethal enough. Now get on over to that car and start crumbling; we're not going home till that hole is plugged."

Truman pulled Myrtle the rest of the way to Danny's car, and they ducked down by the gas cap on the back side.

The shadow puppets on Danny's wall abruptly disappeared, but he could still hear them, even if he couldn't see them. They might as well have knocked on his door to announce their plans.

"We should'a brought gloves," Truman lamented.

"You should'a thought of that before you let me get my fingerprints all over his gas tank. Gas tank, gas chamber, that's where I'm headin', and you the one drivin' me there . . ."

"If I don't get that book back, we might as well both call it quits, 'cause everything is restin' on that. I got a plan, too, ya know . . . secret plan."

"'Top secret' plan, yeah, I know . . . we all got our plans . . ."

She was used to humoring Truman, when he went temporarily insane, and drunk, and his accent became more deep-fried than it had ever been in his childhood.

Truman's fingernails dug into the sugar like a harpy's claws, then began feeding gobs of it into the gas tank. Myrtle scraped away as well, her speed motivated more by the fear of getting caught than by revenge, but they both stopped when they heard the first sizzle as the sugar melted into the gas.

It was working.

"Maybe there's something to this, get his tank all gummed up . . . gotta give you credit," Myrtle said.

"Serves him right. He'll be out here pumpin' the clutch like an idiot, we'll be makin' an end run in his house to get back my book . . ."

Inside his house, Danny was too hypnotized by the absurdity of what they were doing to stop it.

"I'm gettin' light-headed, this gas is makin' me sick," Truman whispered.

Good, serves him right, Danny thought. It was the smell he faced at the pumps every day of his life, the way his head felt all the time, like it was going to float off his body.

"Maybe we should get somebody to break his legs instead . . . serve him right for BREAKING MY SPIRIT . . ." Truman stood up and yelled it at the house, no attempt to keep quiet now.

Myrtle yanked him back down. The fumes were going to her head, too, but she was trying to think straight for a few last minutes.

"If you wanna break something, why not just throw a real brick through his window . . . break in and get your book back that way . . ."

But Truman was full of words, not action, and his words were slurring even more as the gas continued to cast its spell. "It's contaminated now. All those pages, all that work . . . if they only knew every drop of blood those pages took, every drop more they're gonna take, they might as well just put me in a hospital right now and open my veins, 'cause that's what it's gonna be like when my swans finally see what I wrote about 'em. They thought I was done when those stories came out, but I was just gettin' started . . ."

"Swans? What swans? What about your snakes?"

"If they were so stupid, so busy preenin' their feathers to know they shouldn'a been tellin' me their secrets, might as well just put those pearl-covered necks of theirs on the choppin' block, my choppin' block, their pearly necks . . ."

"*What* swans? *Whose* necks?" Myrtle demanded.

Danny wanted to know what swans, whose necks, too—maybe they had money. Maybe they'd buy the book, if they were the ones in it. He wanted addresses and phone numbers.

"I'm a writer, what the hell else am I gonna do with all the stories they told me? Just forget 'em? You know any gangsters?" Truman suddenly switched, bringing down the ax on any more talk of swans or necks or stories.

"That takes the cake . . ."—the cake Myrtle was no longer able to bake, by the way—". . . takes the cake, you thinkin' a decent Christian woman like me would know some nefarious character, only 'farious character I know is *you* . . ."

"If there's any nefarious characters to know, believe me, I already know 'em," Truman said, answering his own question, before he began rambling again. "I've seen blood on the walls, Missy, and I've PUT IT ON THE PAGE, don't you ever forget it, don't think I ever made you clean up after THAT . . . thought I was rid of blood and criminals, now they're back . . . thought I was rid of Perry, now he's back and changed his name to DANNY . . ."

Truman screamed it at the house, now standing up and throwing handfuls of sugar at the front yard.

"... just like Perry, turnin' on me, playin' me after I offered him EVERYTHING ... don't even have to go to sleep at night to be haunted by a ghost, 'cause the ghost is RIGHT THERE. I LOVED HIM and this is how he treats me ...."

Truman was crying.

Danny hid behind the bedroom curtains.

He didn't know he'd hurt Truman like that.

Nobody had ever loved him enough to be hurt by him.

Truman slid down the side of the car, spent by his outburst. He barely had enough energy left to squeak out the next question.

"The ghost is right there. Can't you see it?"

Myrtle almost could: the ghost of her Truman.

She took him by the hand, the sugar that was on both their fingers cementing their bond.

"It's time to go home. We'll get your book back somehow. We've done enough damage for tonight."

"Damage has been done to us." Truman jabbed at his heart. "Done to this. Fix this," he said weakly, trying to rally one last battle cry. He wasn't even looking in the direction of Danny's house anymore; he wasn't looking anywhere; his eyes had gone blank.

"C'mon, we're goin' home. I'm gonna make you a cake if I have to chop down my own sugarcane. You need your sugars to pick you up. You need to give Mr. Jack a call in New York ... all this talk about Danny, it's not right. Mr. Jack the one that loves you ...."

Myrtle tried to pull Truman up but he refused to be lifted.

"No, if I go home, she'll come back. He'll come back. Nancy. Perry. They'll all come back. No more ghosts. I can't take anybody else I don't invite ...."

Myrtle plopped back down next to Truman, defeated for the moment. There they were, Ebony and Ivory, propped up against the metal backrest of a rusted-out car, the dark sky and palm trees high around them.

Danny strained to hear them, but heard only silence, until there was a sulfurous spark, a match striking against the asphalt pavement of the street.

"Oh my God, they're gonna blow up my car . . ."

But a few seconds later, there was no explosion, only inhalation, and then a sickly sweet, smoky smell that wafted all the way up to Danny's window. And then, the almost imperceptible sound of lips and tongues touching paper, the crinkle of fire as it caught.

There, by the open gas tank of Mr. Danny's car, Truman and Myrtle were toking up and smoking a joint.

Danny saw a plume of white rise above the far side of his car, like some smoke signal for peace they were offering up. And from sight to sound: he heard high-pitched humming, almost a purr, and soon, the purr developed into song.

"'We're two lost souls, on the highway of life, da duh duh duh duh, no sister or brother' . . . that's from *Damn Yankees*, best show ever. You ever see that show, Myrtle? Never could understand the baseball part, but sure as hell understood the part 'bout sellin' your soul to the devil, 'cause that's what I did, long time 'go . . ."

"You might'a done that, Mr. Truman, but don't go draggin' me down with you . . . ain't no *two* lost souls about it . . . you take away *one* a' them lost souls right now. Any deal you made with the devil, you made it by your lonesome."

"You see the things I seen, you'd sell your soul to the devil, too, just to forget 'em . . ."

Now that Truman had brought the devil into things, it was definitely time to go.

"Come on now, this hell talk's givin' me the munchies. We'll buy some more sugar, get on home, I'll make you a nice fluffy coc'nut cake . . ."

Danny wanted to say wait, take me with you, I want some cake, too, I'm sorry, I didn't know he loved me, I thought he was just using me, but he stayed quiet and hidden. For the first time since the "book-napping," he bothered to look at what was written on the pages, and almost started crying himself.

On the spot, he came up with another plan, a better one, as he looked out the window one last time and watched Ebony and Ivory struggle up from the car.

"You know, Myrtle, you and me, we're just poor lost souls, on the highway of life . . ."

"No," she answered back, not unkindly, "just the highway out of Palm Springs."

—

An hour or so after Truman and Myrtle had finished spying on Danny, he was spying on them, peeping through the window of the house where he used to be a guest. The smell of gas was on his hands and wouldn't come off, from where he'd had to drain his car to start over with a fresh tank of gas. Their sugar trick had worked; he'd have to remember that next time he wanted to keep somebody from making a fast getaway.

He looked inside one window and saw Truman sitting in his office with a black-and-white lined notebook in his hands, just drawing pictures in it.

Danny moved to another window and saw Myrtle bustling around in the kitchen, tearing open a plastic bag of coconut with her teeth and dumping the shreds of sticky white into a bowl to turn into icing. She snatched a few pinches of it in her fingers and sampled it.

She smiled, like it tasted good.

Danny could taste it through the glass of the window.

He went around to the front door and thought, for just a second, about knocking. Maybe he could start all over, go back to that first time when he'd shown up on a service call to fix the AC. But people like him didn't get third or fourth chances like that, so he put Truman's book down instead, weighing it down with the antique iron that served as a doorstop.

Danny didn't know he was bringing back a life. He just thought it was a cash cow he was about to let go of, and it hadn't been easy. But neither was witnessing Truman's declaration of love in the middle of the street, in the middle of the night.

Maybe Danny did have a little bit of a soul after all.

Maybe he thought he could get even more money from Truman by getting back into his good graces.

Maybe he just wanted to keep his teeth, because Truman had paid for all new ones, and Danny knew he'd be coming back on the warpath for those, too. Getting those taken out would hurt a lot more than giving back some book.

Some book.

Maybe Danny was so upset by what he'd seen in the book's pages he didn't know what to do, and just wanted to be rid of the thing.

It would be there all night, and it would be there when Truman woke up in the morning.

Chapter Eleven

Nelle closed her Bible and put it on the bedside table next to her along with her glasses. It usually put her to sleep, reading the Bible, but not tonight. No, tonight The Reverend was holding forth and he wouldn't let go.

She was sitting up in bed with him; a photo of her going to read and write about him, that is. That's what had been inside the latest box, from the cemetery. When she'd gotten home, she'd taken straight to bed, without telling Alice about her latest discovery. She didn't want to scare the poor woman half to death, any more than Nelle herself was scared. It wasn't every day you walked into a cemetery and found something other than the flowers that were supposed to be there, sitting on top of a burial plot. And what had been sitting there Nelle couldn't figure out, any more than the first box.

This new one was built on the same snakebite kit as before, now edged around the bottom on all four sides by pictures of verdant grass, clipped out of a magazine. An elongated snake wove in and out of the grass, up and around one long tombstone; the snake's head rose up, ready to strike, just where the box opened.

There were no names on the tombstone.

On top of the lid, a tiny chestnut horse appeared to rear back on its hind legs, its mane tossing.

And inside that box, tucked underneath grass, and a snake, and a horse, was the photograph Nelle held. Just one this time, and of recent vintage: Nelle walking up the steps of the courthouse in nearby Jefferson City. A big courthouse in the middle of an old-fashioned town square, where friendly old people played checkers and attended trials and didn't care, or even know, that she was famous. Nelle. They didn't even know her last name. She was just another old lady who liked a good true crime, and The Reverend's was as good and true as it got.

Nelle was writing a book about him.

She'd been writing it for years, even though she knew she'd probably never finish it. She just couldn't figure out a way to tell it, even though she knew every in and out of the story. He had used voodoo, or so it was said, to kill off five members of his own family, for the insurance money. Then, having the nerve to preach at one of their funerals, he'd finally been killed himself, shot by a grieving relative and literally falling into the coffin.

It was the deep calling the deep, yet again.

She'd been hesitant to even start taking notes at first, not sure she wanted to go back to the realm of murder that had started with Truman. But she couldn't resist evil, or, more precisely, trying to sort out what caused it. Evil had to be punished. She could do that with her writing, even if it didn't always happen in real life.

Her writing.

That brought a sad laugh to her.

It was never going to happen, same as it wasn't going to happen for Truman.

What had happened to them in Kansas? Had those murders so sapped them they didn't have anything left over to put on the page?

She used to try, because she wanted to bring justice to the people The Reverend had killed. But ever since Truman's first call, nights ago, a new and different thought had come to her: did The Reverend's victims want her help with justice? Or would they rather the whole thing, the crimes committed years ago, just vanish, so they could be left in peace, to go on with their lives of anonymity? Is that what the surviving Clutter children, the two grown-up girls who were out of the house that night, would have wanted? Had she and Truman done right by them?

Who knows; they never bothered to ask.

Who knows, indeed?

Nancy Clutter did. She'd just told Truman he needn't have bothered; she hadn't wanted the fame.

Nancy said what had been on Nelle's mind for the last twenty-five years.

Nelle ripped the photo in her hands in half, to drown out the sound of someone else saying:

I've got you in my sights.

You can't escape me.
I'm never far away.
I know where you go.
The Reverend isn't important.
It's you I want.

—

Nelle wanted as far away from that cemetery and its pictures as sleep would take her, but dreams wouldn't come. They remained far away, displaced by waking images of tombstones and snake men and ugly plastic flowers on graves, trembling walks toward coffins and a mother and brother lying flat and still and a Reverend who offered death instead of comfort.

Maybe those *were* her dreams.

They were all crowding her head, until a ghost showed up and shooed them all away.

Nelle was looking out her bedroom window at a perfectly round moon. That's strange, she thought; she'd looked at the almanac, and it hadn't predicted a full moon. She reached to the bedside table and patted down the objects on it until she came to her glasses; she picked them up by the stems, careful not to smear the glass with fingerprints. She put them on; it took a few seconds to adjust to what she thought was the light of the full moon.

Instead, she decided it must be a yellow smiley-face balloon that had floated out of someone's hand and gotten entangled in the tree branches outside her window. She smiled to herself at the revelation, although she wished it was the moon. She needed a moon right now. *I'll be looking at the moon, but I'll be seeing you,* she thought; *I'll be looking at the moon, but I'll be seeing a smiley face,* just didn't have the same ring.

And then she did see a smiley face, in her room. Smiling at her. She stopped breathing.

She tried to pull air into her lungs to yell for Alice, but couldn't. She couldn't think, let alone breathe. It wouldn't matter anyway; Alice wouldn't hear a peep because she barely heard anything anymore, except what she wanted to.

One of Truman's crooks was in Nelle's room to be her dispatcher. It was an automatic response: one of her hands flew to her throat, the other reached to the bedside Bible to ask the angels to watch over her, to not let death hurt, whenever, however it came.

Maybe she could let the intruder have whatever he'd come to steal, and he'd leave. (He'd already stolen her life and pasted it on a box; what else was there to take?) But bargaining like that—here, take what you want and leave, I won't tell—never worked. It's what the Clutters had tried, and look what happened to them.

The person in her room was in no hurry; he was just watching and waiting.

So was Nelle. She saw a flare of red, but it wasn't blood: it blossomed, crinkled into ashy gray and white, like a firework dying in the sky, then blossomed red again.

It was the draw on a cigarette. She knew it well. She craved it, after a three-pack-a-day habit.

Her intruder was smoking.

Then another pull, another flame of red, and the face behind the cigarette was illuminated.

Now she knew who it was.

Kenyon Clutter, the boy she'd only ever seen in photographs.

Kenyon, the four-eyed geek with the strange name, who'd never gotten to make love, who had to watch his father cower before a madman, who couldn't see a thing without his glasses, including his own murder.

Kenyon, who was so lucky he was blind.

He was the Clutter Nelle had loved the most, after trying to love them all. Truman had given all his love to Nancy; there wasn't any room left to love her. That's the grave he'd made a beeline for, nobody else's. That's who he gave the last scene in his book to, nobody else. A young girl, cut down in her prime, wearing the same red velvet dress in her coffin she'd planned to wear to her prom. Nelle wanted to feel for Nancy, she really did—Nelle had gotten to have her prom, after all, as ugly and ungainly as she'd felt at it—but no . . .

It was Kenyon who had somehow taken the most of her grief and left her very little to spare.

After a love as strange as that, she didn't think he was here to kill her, so she let herself breathe again. And the first and only thing she wanted in that first intake of air was nicotine, to anesthetize the terror she'd just felt. Her heart wouldn't stop beating out of her chest until she had a smoke.

She propped herself up on her pillow and asked the ghost of Kenyon Clutter if she could bum a cigarette.

He said sure, and held out the pack.

Asking a ghost for a cancer stick.

Now she knew there was a first for everything, for every absurd thing under the sun, just as she knew she was entering the land of no return, where her friend Truman Capote had gone to permanently reside. At first, when he'd told her about his ghosts, she'd laughed. Then she'd felt strangely jealous. Now, she felt even.

She felt chosen.

She felt alive.

She felt lost, and wondered if she'd ever be found again.

Kenyon slid a bony wrist out from the heavy cotton sleeve of his letter sweater. It was hard to see the color in the dark room, but Nelle thought it was maroon. She'd seen the letter sweater in his closet back in Kansas, but she couldn't remember precisely. Maroon, wasn't it, with a gold letter? For basketball? Or was it 4-H? Did they give letters for 4-H? She couldn't believe she'd forgotten.

The hand did a precise little shake; a cigarette popped out of the pack, already lit. Either Kenyon moved faster than the human eye could see, with a lighter in his other hand, or he'd just done something that was humanly impossible.

But possible for him, because he wasn't human anymore.

Neither was Nelle.

She didn't know what she was anymore, except . . . adrift.

Nelle sucked in the offered cigarette, trying to get her brain to kick-start, trying to get the nicotine to calm her nerves and slow her breathing and heart, and make her wake up.

This couldn't be happening.

This was happening.

This is what Kenyon had felt, this jangled panic, just before . . .

She had to stop it.

"How's Nancy? How's your sister?"

Nelle knew it was the dumbest thing she'd ever said the minute she heard it. Dumber even than saying she wanted to be the Jane Austen of south Alabama. (Why south Alabama? Why not all of Alabama, why limit herself? That was dumb.)

No, this was dumb, remembering an old interview she'd given, when a figment smoking a cigarette was in her bedroom, and she was smoking with it.

It.

Him.

Kenyon.

"Why does everybody always ask about her first? Nancy. Just cuz she's a girl. Like it hurt her more. I got it too, ya know. Why don't you ask me how I am? Murder hurts the same, boy or girl. Hurts like hell."

He angrily dashed his cigarette to the floor and ground it out.

Nelle remembered her manners and did what he'd asked. "I'm sorry. How are you?"

"Okay. That's all I wanted. To be asked." Kenyon lit another cigarette, trying to calm himself down. "And I'm sorry, too. It only hurt for a sec. Not even that. I didn't even feel it." He looked down, searching with his eyes, his foot. "And don't worry 'bout your floor. It won't leave a mark. Trust me."

Nelle knew it wouldn't, because she knew Kenyon wasn't really there. This was just a dream, about a smiley-face balloon, and cigarettes, and cemeteries, and The Reverend, and Kenyon Clutter. The clutter of a dream . . .

So why did she smell smoke?

No matter if she and Alice had nothing to talk about at breakfast the next morning, she would never tell Alice about this.

But she was wrong about the smiley face, she saw now in the glow of the cigarette. Smiley faces had strong, definite features: assertive, contagious black smiles, coal-button eyes. Kenyon had none of those: his features were haggard, washed-out; his lips had no color at all. They were creamy, pale, dry; his eyes looked the same behind his thick glasses, as pale and wispy as the cigarette smoke that came out his nostrils. There was so much pomade in his hair it looked wispy white as well, peppery and gray and silver. He was only fifteen, but his hair had no color at all, like a very old man's.

There was so much Nelle wanted to know: about the Clutters, about Kansas, about Heaven. That is where Kenyon had gone, wasn't it, and where he'd come from now? He deserved that much, didn't he, eternal rest, after what he'd gone through?

Where did she even start?

At the beginning.

Truman.

"Truman said . . . were you really at Truman's the other night, like he said? Did you see him? I couldn't tell if he was just dreaming, or . . ."

Kenyon finished her thought, lifting an imaginary bottle to his mouth. He wasn't big on words.

"He called me up, just outta his mind, and said he'd seen a ghost . . ."

"He . . . he shouldn't drink so much. Or take all those pills. I mean, I know he's your friend and everything . . ."

"Not so much anymore . . ."

". . . but . . . it's addin' up. Gonna take its toll. Actually, it's not that long till . . ."

He stopped short, realizing he was about to spill privileged information.

Nelle jumped on it.

"D'you know? Can you see what's gonna take me? Or when?"

"Can't say."

"Can't, or won't?"

Now the woman who was known for her lush words and great descriptive powers was becoming as sullen and tight-lipped, as stingy with words, as the high school boy who wasn't standing in her room, sucking on a cig.

"Sorry. Not allowed."

He put his thumb and index finger together, next to his pale, creamy lips, and twisted the lock closed on the answer.

So be it. She had tried. She didn't really want to know how she was going to go. She didn't even want to know about her death after it happened, like Kenyon evidently did, having to remember it all the time.

He read her mind again and shrugged.

"Yeah, I know. Bum luck."

Bum luck. A short life, a horrible death, and that's what it came down to. Bum luck. It wasn't eloquent, but it pretty much summed things up, Nelle thought.

Kenyon was better with words than he thought.

He fashioned his hand into a gun shape—forefinger out, thumb up—pointed it between his eyes, and then cocked and pulled an imaginary trigger.

"Kkkaaaboooommmmmmm . . ."

He made a high-school-boy sound effect, magnifying the finale over and over, and fell back into her mirror.

The mirror shook.

Nelle's reflection rattled in it.

Ghosts didn't have the weight and mass to knock into something and make it rattle.

Kenyon looked at Nelle and again seemed to know what she was thinking. How could he explain himself, what he was now? Ghost, dream, visitation, imagining? She was the one in the room with the words smart and good enough to do it. But Kenyon struggled on with the only words he did have.

"Sorry, that wasn't nice, the gun thing. It just kinda . . . sticks with ya. Let's change the subject."

"Fine with me."

She'd like to change the dream, but that didn't seem possible. *Was* it a dream?

She tried to smell him without him noticing, tried to pass it off like she was just inhaling the smoke from her cigarette, that fine vintage of tar and nicotine and tobacco. But it was his pomade she got instead, to let her know how real he seemed.

He smelled like the boys she'd gone to college with, the artistic types who'd worked on the school humor magazine with her. The ones who shyly asked her for dates, the ones she always told no.

Why hadn't she ever said yes?

She would have said yes to Kenyon Clutter.

She took another whiff, for courage, and asked what was really on her mind:

"Why did Truman send those boxes? It is Truman, isn't it? Then who's following me around, taking those pictures, trying to scare me? I don't want this. I don't want attention. Truman does, but not me."

Kenyon wasn't answering her question.

"Am I missing something? Just give me a hint. Am I supposed to do something? Is he *mad*? Are *you* mad? We tried to get your story right, I swear we did. Nancy—is she mad? Truman said she was . . ."

Nelle was running at the mouth now, every question, every thought, bubbling over at last. So was Kenyon. He didn't have much time left.

"Yeah, but . . . she'll get over it. No matter what Nancy says, everybody wants to be remembered. I wanted to make things, build things, maybe become an architect." He took one last, sad drag, then ground that cigarette out, too. "I wanted to make so much more."

"So did I," Nelle thought. "I've had all this time, but . . . have I wasted it?"

Of all the questions she'd asked Kenyon Clutter, this was the one she most wanted answered, and she couldn't answer it herself. "I've had so much time, and you had no time at all, you poor boy . . ."

He was fading away, his smell of smoke and greasy kid stuff disappearing to just a grace note, the reflection of the moon off his eyeglasses to just a speck, the maroon of his letter sweater melding into the indistinguishable dark of the room.

Nelle closed her eyes at the very moment she should be opening them widest, trying to take in every last vestige of him; she tightened her brain and eyes to squeeze him back, she even yelled out, "Don't go yet . . ."

But he was gone.

When Nelle woke up in the morning, had she remembered anything from the night, she'd have seen that Kenyon had indeed kept his word: the cigarettes he'd stubbed out on her floor hadn't made any marks at all.

But the cigarette in her ashtray—she really shouldn't smoke at night.

Chapter Twelve

When Truman woke up after the night of trying to sugar-bomb Danny's car, he remembered this, from a night of horrible dreams: he had been held down and told he was going to have both arms amputated, above the elbow at the bicep. He couldn't see who was doing it, but he felt that they were strong and that there was no resisting them. Broad cuffs of leather were tightened around his limbs; his saggy old-man flesh squeezed under the restraints, and knives were sharpened. Whoever was doing it gave him an injection just above the leather cuff; he twisted and fought against that as much as the approaching blade.

He passed out before the first cut, because he knew what the result would be: he would have no hands or fingers to write with anymore.

Waking up extra early, Truman couldn't remember ever crying so much; his pillow was soaked to the touch, tears and snot tracing the outline of his face.

Walking his dog that morning was a blessing; he never wanted to go to sleep again as long as he lived.

———

Outside, on the porch, Truman's jowly bulldog, Maggie, saw the manuscript first, and squatted to pee on something that had once held her master's scent.

Truman shooed the dog away, at first thinking somebody had dropped off a manuscript for him to read. They did it all the time: *What do you think of this? Can you help me get it published? Would you just jot down a few notes? What do I do now?* Truman was happy to let Maggie pee and poop on those books; sometimes he felt like joining in, then telling their owners exactly what he had done. He wasn't in the business of getting someone else's books published when he could barely finish one of his own anymore.

But these pages were somehow different; Truman knew that the second Maggie finished and began licking the spot she had started to pee on just seconds before. Truman would know these pages anywhere; they were the exact height of the stack of pages that had sat next to his typewriter for years, with the same familiar smudges and dog-ears marking them. But the only way they could have gotten there is if Danny had returned them, and people like Danny didn't change their minds.

Did they?

Danny had tried to murder Truman by taking his book, and now he was returning it? It didn't make sense. Truman knew the criminal mind, and making amends wasn't in its repertoire. You couldn't take back murder, no matter how much you tried, and that's what this abduction had amounted to—murder. Danny was the type to try to make a mint off someone else's misery, just like Dick and Perry had. Perry had even tried to sell Truman's letters to him, a hustler till the very last minute he was swinging from a rope. If he could have, Perry would have cut the rope down after he was dead and tried to sell that as well.

What if Danny had defaced the pages? Truman was almost afraid to look. But he bent down and lifted off the antique iron doorstop that had kept them from blowing away in the night—the same iron, now rusted to a flaky pumpkin orange, that his old cousin Sook used to put on top of a hot stove, then do up their clothes with.

Truman looked at the first page, and it was what he remembered, and he looked at the second page, and he remembered that, too, and he looked at the very last page, some hundreds of pages behind the first and the second, and that was the same. He fanned through them all, and there was no excrement or blood wiped on them—except what Truman himself had left there, sweated out in his writing, to mark them as his own.

He had been spared; his arms hadn't been cut off in the night, but returned to him. The nightmare had been his penance, what could happen if he wasn't anymore respectful of his gift. But he had been the stronger; the surgeons hadn't been able to complete their cutting. Truman still had his arms, his hands, his instrument.

He still had his gift.

He went inside, completely forgetting that Maggie was still out, doing her business.

Truman had business of his own to finish, now that his life had been returned.

He needed somewhere to hide the book so no one could ever take it again.

———

When Myrtle came to work that morning, mere hours after she'd left from baking her cake, she found Maggie pawing and scratching at the screen door, and Truman inside, oblivious and manic, scrubbing snake (and Danny) off the walls of his inner sanctum.

It was the first time Myrtle had ever seen him do anything, other than drink, or try to write.

Truman looked at her, his eyes full of something she hadn't seen in a very long time.

"I've got it," he said triumphantly.

Myrtle said, "No, I think you missed a little spot over there."

"It. My book. My revenge," he said.

Truman held up the stack of pages, but Myrtle still thought he was talking about something else. There was something strange about the way he said "it."

"I feel like I've been given back my arms. Do you know what that's like, losing your arms then getting them reattached? And now my arms are gonna reach out into the world and shake their teeth loose, molar by molar. This . . ."

. . . and there Truman raised up the pages even higher, like an evangelist in a summer revival tent, shaking the pages like he was shaking the devil out of their very souls . . .

". . . this is what they want but they're not gonna get it. Oh, no, I've got a special place for this," he said. "A special place indeed. Danny must have brought it back when he saw that I was a force to reckon with."

"We were a force, all right; that box of confectioners' sugar must have had him quaking in his boots."

Myrtle grabbed the sponge Truman had been using, dipped it in a bucket of Lysol, and started scrubbing away at a dab of dried snake. She rubbed so hard the wallpaper tore away; what had been Truman's eyes from the Warhol print gave way to bare wall underneath.

Truman must have had some of her coconut cake for breakfast; sugar was speeding him on, and he could barely slow down as he put aside the pages and moved his attention to a new snake box, the glue still drying on it. "I started working on this the minute I got the book back, when I wasn't washing off snake. You ever see a snake fight? I have. Two of 'em, back behind Mr. Katz's drug store when I was just six years old. Imagine an adult taking a child, an impressionable child, to see that, but that's what my aunt Tiny did. Cost a quarter each. We begged to go, she took us. Me and my friend Nelle Harper, they killed each other."

"The snakes?"

He didn't answer, seemingly lost to the past, and who had killed whom.

"That's when I decided what I wanted to be when I grew up. A snake charmer. Just another name for writer. Keep the snakes from fighting. That's who you gotta send this to. Nelle Harper. She'll know what I mean. She'll remember."

The scene on the box looked somehow outdoorsy, but Myrtle couldn't really tell what it was, just what looked like a wonderful carpet of green to walk barefoot through. She curled up her toes inside her shoes, trying to feel it.

"That your Garden of Earthly De-lights again?" she asked, not quite approvingly. There was something a little bit sinful about it, she thought, like man trying to re-create what God had already made, a whole lot better.

"Um-hum," Truman answered, with the same kind of teasing excitement he used to have when he was writing, when he'd work so nonstop his clothes would go dirty and smelly in the pursuit of his art.

Maybe the boxes were his new art.

He was always talking about "new forms"; maybe this was one of them. Myrtle got confused when he talked about things like that, and usually excused herself to go do a load of laundry. Leave him to his new forms; leave her to her laundry.

Truman smoothed down a final leaf of grass that he'd pasted on the box, edged out an air bubble that had pimpled up, then wiped a smear of glue off on his shirt and moved his attention to a stack of pictures Myrtle had never seen before, kept in an old brown accordion file tied together with a fraying black shoelace. Inside, there were dozens and dozens of photographs: real pictures of real people, not torn out of magazines or art books.

Truman paused, debating among several small black-and-white candids, then chose one: it showed four people bundled up in coats against the cold, as if they were trapped inside a snow globe. He tenderly placed it inside the box, as if he were trying to warm the people up, deep inside the leafy tropical forest he had created for them on the outside.

Myrtle leaned in closer to get a better look, but Truman

slammed the lid closed before she could, as if he had to get the photo in the box before he changed his mind.

Changed his mind about what, she didn't know.

—

Now she knew.

Myrtle stood in line at the post office, expecting a big pair of hands to clamp down on her meaty shoulders at any minute. Because of what was in the package she held, she thought the smell might draw flies, and flies, looks, and looks, arrest. She'd wrapped the box herself, after Truman relinquished it to her custody, with a double and then triple layer of brown butcher paper. She'd even baptized it with some of the White Shoulders bath powder Truman gave her every year for Christmas. But as she stood in line, she thought that would have to be some mighty strong perfume to stanch the smell of an animal that had laid out in the Palm Springs sun for days on end, then been scraped off a wall and put inside a box.

Myrtle told Truman, "You can't go sendin' dead things through the U.S. Postal Service."

He said, "I've been around enough dead things in my life to know what I can and cannot do with them. Mail it."

But no one was wrinkling up their nose funny in her direction, or sneaking off to call the police. She was safe for now, that is, unless her picture popped up on a wanted poster. She was almost afraid to look up at the bulletin board where the FBI posters were—usually, one of her favorite pastimes in the PO—because she was afraid she'd see her face staring right back at her. What if someone had seen her and Truman out at Mr. Danny's last night, tampering with his gas tank? She could just imagine the mug shot they'd take of that: a picture of the both of them, beaming the silly, hungry grins of two fools high on gas fumes and doobies, who had the munchies for homemade coconut cake.

Slowly, so as not to draw attention, she let her glance move from the package in her hands to the bulletin board.

So far, so good: the FBI hadn't caught up with Myrtle J. Bennett. She could breathe.

But then she caught a whiff of snake.

She panicked and looked straight ahead again, to divert attention.

Why didn't Truman have her mail off one of his butterflies, then they'd both be safe.

He loved butterflies.

He had collections of them all over his house, "butterflies under glass" he called them, exotic breeds mounted on black velvet and encased under Plexiglas, or swimming inside clear glass paperweights.

Myrtle didn't understand how you could love something so much, then have it killed and preserved so you could stare at it forever, no matter how pretty it was. But Truman said butterflies had a short life span and were going to die anyway. They were going to get old and tired, their high and proud wings go limp, their color fade and rub off to gray, so why not capture them at the peak of their powers, when their wings were full and strong, all their colors still intact?

He said it exactly like that, all those words.

She wondered if he was just talking about butterflies.

Sometimes, he called her "his black butterfly"; that's what she had been, in the Cotton Club. A butterfly, hard to see it now with her ham-hock arms and flat feet, but she'd been spry on the wing umpteen years ago in Harlem. No penguin suit for her, no sir; she'd had a costume none of the other girls could carry off, gossamer wings of real spun gold edged in black, and streaks of gold glitter on her cheeks. She caressed her body with the wings, then tipped them through the smoky air of the club to some lucky gentleman in the audience. Reached out and blessed him with the wing of her costume, and then flitted away.

She sometimes thought that's why Truman had hired her, because she'd been a butterfly in another life.

Something as pretty as a butterfly wouldn't set off a stink.

The post office line inched forward, and Myrtle began thinking about the lady who was getting the package, on the other end of the receiving line. It was the same lady Truman had taken to calling late at night, when his ghosts came. How would she feel when she opened up this package, all excited, thinking it was a present—that's how Myrtle felt when she got something wrapped up in the mail—then, surprise, it's snake guts! Should Myrtle call her up and warn her? Or better yet, not send it at all, just tell Truman she had? No, she was a lot of things, but she wasn't a liar. She'd say a prayer for the name on the address; that would have to be good enough, until Truman helped her open her maid service.

Then she'd make all the damn calls she wanted.

She closed her eyes to pray, but the hum of the overhead fluorescent lights changed what she had to say. Instead of saying "Thank you, God," and leaving it at that, she said "Thank you, God, for the post office." Maybe that was her new form of prayer, just like the box she was holding was Truman's new way of writing.

If not her prayer, it was certainly her secret: coming here late some nights, on her way home from work. You'd think after a hard day at Truman's, she'd just want to get on home to her husband, but there was even more work waiting for her there—fixing his dinner, talking to him, when they'd said all they had to say years ago. No, the post office was the only place she could be alone, even if it *was* under the "cold, clinical glare"—that's a phrase she picked up from Truman—of the fluorescents. She liked the hum and hiss they made; it filled her head and she didn't have to think anymore. She liked background noise when it was as soft as that. She liked the idea of a government building that wasn't locked up but was free and open to the public, like the front section where all the PO boxes and copy machine were. She paid her taxes like anybody else; she had a right to see what they were being used for, any hour of the day or night. She liked the big marble counter in the middle of the room, and all the forms that were tucked into it. She always took some, whether she needed them or not; her tax dollars paid for those, too.

Myrtle J. Bennett liked getting her money's worth.

In a public building where anyone could walk in on her at any moment, she found the most comfort and privacy.

It had started when she went there to do some copying for Truman on their Xerox machine, ten cents a copy. She'd done it for a few nights in a row, but when he stopped writing, and didn't have anything else left to copy, she found herself still going there.

She couldn't accept it on its own, at first; she didn't understand the draw of the place. Being there had to have a purpose, an activity—so she Xeroxed her face. She lifted up the heavy rubber cover and laid her cheek against the cool glass of the machine, then dropped in a dime and squinted her eyes shut against the luminous green light that whirred to life to take her picture.

The first night she did it, she took her picture and ran. She didn't know what had gotten into her. And how stupid she'd been—she'd left a big greasy streak on the glass where her face had been.

It was as good as a fingerprint.

She went back the very same night, armed with Windex, to wipe it off.

As soon as she realized she could get rid of the evidence, she did it again: put her head down on the glass, almost like she was taking a nap, closed her eyes, and waited. The light felt so warm on her cheek, she didn't want to wake up. She always wiped down the plate glass when she left, so nobody else would get the idea of doing it, too.

This was hers and hers alone, and soon enough, it might be the only record that she'd been here at all.

By now, she had a regular gallery of portraits: The Many Moods of Myrtle, she liked to call them. The photos showed every squishy, haggard line in her face, but she embraced them as works of art, badges of honor. Rather than avoid the age lines, she tried to divine her future in them, see on her face what most fortune tellers would look to her palms for.

With what she suspected was bad news on the way, she needed to see what the future held.

—

Myrtle heard the word "Next," then felt a nudge in her back and opened her eyes.

She wasn't having her picture taken, as she'd been daydreaming away, but standing in the slow-boat-to-China line at the PO. She stumbled up to the clerk and handed over the package.

Let it be that other woman's burden now; Myrtle had burdens enough of her own, and was glad to get rid of it.

The cashier weighed it, stamped it, and dumped it in an outgoing bin, without ever looking up.

Myrtle was safe: no one had sniffed out her secrets, her snake in the box or her night life at the post office.

She was safe, for now.

For now, until the next stop she had to make.

Chapter Thirteen

Another box, another coffin, another picture had come.

And something else, something that had once been alive: a piece of skeleton, shreds of flesh still adhering to the rings of a snake's rattle.

Thank God Nelle had been at the front door when it came; if Alice had opened this package, Nelle would be looking for a new housemate.

This would have killed her.

Nelle sat at her desk, four newly revealed objects lined up in front of her, from largest to smallest, container to contained: the decorated snakebite kit; the tiny, hand-carved coffin that had been inside; a photograph; and snake remains. If these things were supposed to tell her something, add up to something, she had no clue what.

For the first time, there was something dead, the snake; would the deliveries keep escalating in that direction, until the dead thing was her? Truman wasn't a killer; he *wrote* about killers, or he and Nelle had together, once upon a time. Was he warning her that she was about to be killed by someone? Someone he had hired, whom it was too late to call off? Some other assassin, whose plot Truman had uncovered? What if Truman wasn't behind the packages at all? What if it was The Reverend? He had killed not once, but five times; he could kill again . . .

. . . except he was already dead.

Sorry.

Focus.

WHY was somebody doing this? She hadn't done anything to hurt anybody. Hadn't they read her book? This was just like killing a mockingbird, all over again. A mockingbird didn't hurt anybody . . .

Sorry.

Focus.

She pushed the first two snake boxes and their contents to the side, then brought the newest addition to the edge of the desk. The objects at hand, literally—her hands shook as she touched each one in turn, trying to fit the puzzle pieces into some kind of order that made sense.

The collage on the newest box seemed like a continuation of the previous one, the one that had been buried at Ed's grave. A photo of an ancient tombstone, into which the beatific face of a Victorian cherub had been carved, was on the front, but a separate panel, a sort of hieroglyphics, had been pasted over where the name should be. On the lid of the box, positioned as if looking down at the tombstone, were two figures—a boy and girl from the 1920s, paper dolls with idyllic, smiling faces. Just out of view on the back of the box, as if it were sneaking up on the children, was a drawing of a snake's head, its mouth stretched open, baring fangs and a slithering tongue. And on one of the side panels, another horse, with a man's naked torso stretched out on top, as if riding it.

Nelle wanted to ball up her fist and smash it down on the thing.

It was pornographic.

If this was Truman's handiwork, he could go to Hell.

She'd never wished that on anyone.

Was the box supposed to say something about their ill-fated meeting at Nancy Clutter's grave, to which Truman had ridden Nancy's horse? There wasn't any snake there, unless you counted Truman.

—

He'd gone missing, and Nelle had found him, on a horse, at the grave plot where the Clutters were buried.

Truman had never been on a horse in his life.

It was their second trip to Kansas, weeks after the murders. Truman hadn't been able to bring himself there any earlier. When Nelle asked what he was doing, he said he'd found out this was what Nancy did all the time; it was even Nancy's horse, Babe, that he'd ridden there. "I wanted to see what it felt like. Makes me think she was a lonely girl."

"Makes me think she was a scary girl."

This was years before Nelle would come to find solace in the same kinds of trips, years before people would start calling Nelle a scary girl, too.

Then, the Clutters' graves were still fresh, four long mounds of dirt covered by a light dusting of snow. Soon enough, they'd be completely covered, by the winter storm that had been predicted. Truman would be there through that storm and many more before the book would be finished; he would make many more solitary visits, through every season, to that graveyard.

The horse bent down and nudged its snout at Nancy's grave, as if it knew its mistress was there. If Truman had described it to Nelle instead of her seeing it with her very own eyes, she wouldn't have believed it.

"If you put that in the book, nobody'll believe you," she said.

"I've got you as my witness."

As the horse moved around, nosing its snout at the other graves—maybe it was just rooting for food, pasture to graze on, and happened to pick Nancy's grave first—Truman said, "It's perfect. Better than I imagined. I won't have snow coming down, of course, it's gotta be spring, the time of rebirth, but this is where Alvin Dewey and Susan Kidwell will meet in the last chapter . . ."

"Susan Kidwell?"

"Nancy's best friend. She and Dewey separately come here to lay flowers. They're moving on with their lives. Saying good-bye . . ."

"You can't do that."

"Why not?"

"It didn't happen."

"But it's dramatic. It's perfect. I'm using it."

Nelle tried to keep her voice calm.

"After all the work you've gone to, that *we've* gone to . . . trying to keep everything real, all the interviews we've done, the people we've met, they trust us . . . you can't lie like that."

"It's my book. I can do whatever I please."

She swore she'd heard him say the very same thing when he was just six years old.

"You cannot do that to the Clutters."

"I don't see them here to stop me."

"I do."

She saw their four graves, and a horse nudging at them in the snow.

Nelle continued, "If you put that scene in, I'll tell people not to talk to you anymore. I'm the one gets 'em buttered up. I'm the one they trust."

"If you dare tell people not to talk to me, I'll take you off the list . . ."

That was his weapon, as much as the gun and knife Dick and Perry had used.

". . . I won't invite you to my party . . ."

He'd barely begun the book, but was already planning the biggest party the world had ever seen to celebrate it.

Black and white, just like the bleak landscape of a cemetery covered in snow.

He put the scene in the book.

—

Without her realizing it, Nelle's hand had tightened around the box, and was squeezing the very life out of it. For an aging lady with arthritis, her grip was amazingly strong. She watched the figures of the tiny boy and girl collapse in on themselves, as if disappearing into a sinkhole . . .

But she couldn't do it.

She couldn't crush herself, destroy her childhood, and she felt sure that's what Truman—*somebody*—meant the figures to represent.

She took an extra-long breath, flexed her hand open and shut to get the feeling back, then moved on to the next object in front of her: the tiny coffin. She nudged its lid open; the inside was lined. It wasn't pink satin, like her mother's coffin, or white, like her brother's, but red velvet—like the dress in which Nancy Clutter had been buried, the dress she and Susan Kidwell had just finished making before . . . The velvet in Nelle's tiny coffin wasn't new, but soiled and tattered, the plush worn down to a bare sheen, the purpley-blue color of blood under the skin, instead of red.

Nelle's hand jerked away: had the velvet actually come from Nancy Clutter's dress? Had someone actually dug up her body and snatched a piece of cloth from the beautiful dress covering it? Not even Truman would have gone that far.

Would he?

Had Truman become a grave robber?

It couldn't be from Nancy's grave; it couldn't. It couldn't . . .

Breathe.

Focus.

Nestled inside the coffin, on top of the worn velvet, had been a single photograph.

At first, Nelle didn't realize she was staring at a group portrait that included herself: it could have been any four strangers, bundled up against the cold. But one of the four was a giant, and another a virtual midget, a scarf coiled around his neck so thick it looked like a snake strangling him.

Nelle had to smile, now and then; she—the giantess in the picture—had warned Truman that that scarf would be the death of him. People in Kansas didn't wear scarves like that, no matter how cold it got. Harold Nye, one of the Kansas Bureau of Investigation agents, and his wife, Joyce, sandwiched between Truman and Nelle, were used to cold weather; they didn't have to wrinkle up their faces and squeeze their eyes against it, as Nelle did in the picture. But even with the cold, their faces were expectant, their eyes shining and dancing, their smiles open and wide, and their teeth gleaming—or maybe they were just chattering.

This time, at least, Nelle remembered who was on the other side of the camera: Ray Cosgrove, the teenage bellhop from their hotel, whom Truman had hired to play chauffeur for the night. He took the picture with Truman's own little Brownie camera, and shot it at an angle that revealed a patch of the sidewalk behind the four of them. Nelle could see their footprints in the snow, muddied and overlapping, leading from the restaurant to the car.

It would be the longest night of her life, but it would have nothing to do with ghosts—except the ghost of the girl she used to be, long before Truman called and introduced his ghosts to her.

—

It was the night at the end of a very long day, during which they had come face to face with the twenty crime-scene photos for the first time.

Nelle had had to grip a desk and force herself to breathe when she looked at those, too.

Photos so gruesome she had tried to turn their reality into vague, abstract shapes: turn pools of blood into fluid circles on a field of black and white, turn bodies and faces into geometry, not people whose names she now knew, who had been spared no dignity in death—and no further dignity as she and Truman bore witness to the last, and most intimate, moment of their lives.

Truman picked picked picked at the coroner, wanting to go inside the photographs. He wanted to travel inside the gunshots, speed with the bullets through flesh, and feel what the bullets had felt, the resistance that bone and cartilage and brain had offered. He wanted the perfect word to describe it—not *scared* or *petrified*; those were easy, obvious words—but a word of tactility and feeling, like *hot* or *sharp*; he wanted to stack words on top of words on the page to convey the 3-D, split-second immediacy and chaos of what had happened.

Truman wanted to know what absolute fear felt like.

He lobbed question after question at the coroner to get the answer:

—How much adrenaline?

—How fast were their hearts racing?

—Was their breath hot or cold?

—Did the fear anesthetize them?

—Could they feel anything?

Question after question, with split-second rapidity, but at the end of it all, after a torrent of words, there were still no answers.

The coroner had to admit he had never been shot to death, so he couldn't honestly describe how it felt.

And that's what Truman wanted: honesty.

That thing in death, their deaths, that he had never had in his life.

———

At the end of that long day, and their session with the coroner, Nelle was spent. Never shy about talking, she felt as if she couldn't form another word for another soul, or keep her ears open a second longer to hear conversation in return. By five o'clock that day, it was dark outside. Downtown, merchants' hands reached into windows and exchanged Open signs for ones that read Closed. Shades were pulled down, and newly installed metal grates slid across plate glass doors.

That had never happened, before the killings.

Nelle told Truman she was going to do the same, put out her Closed sign, and pull down her shades until the alarm clock rang the next morning.

"I can't talk to another person about this damn murder. Tonight is a night off from violence; I declare a moratorium on the very mention of it, until tomorrow morning—at the earliest."

Every night, Nelle and Truman gathered in his hotel room, next door to hers, to review the separate interviews they had conducted during the day. They didn't use tape recorders, or take notes while they were talking to people; that would have scared them away. They took notes only in their heads, as Truman had taught Nelle to do when she was just five years old. He'd had her in training to be the good assistant ever since then. Truman claimed to have 93 percent accuracy in his recall; it's that other 7 percent that should have been a warning to them all.

But not tonight. Nelle wanted to talk, or think—or not think—about anything that *wasn't* the Clutters, or Kansas corn-fields. She didn't want to talk at all, but Truman had other plans for her.

"Oh, no, Ma'am Missy, we're hittin' the town tonight, and takin' the Nyes with us. So shinny and skinny back to the hotel, soak in a tub full of bubbles, then get up and dress nice, 'cause I'm takin' you out for the surprise of your life."

Since she'd just seen pictures of a house where the blood of four people still coated the baseboards, it must be some surprise.

"Truman, not tonight, I'm dead . . ."

"So are the Clutters, so don't ever use that expression again unless you really mean it. Now start soakin' and don't fall asleep or you'll drown in the tub. I don't wanna get my hands all pruney dippin' 'em in just to save you."

And thus would begin their longest night together.

—

At her house, Joyce Nye was as ebullient as Nelle was despondent: a night out with Capote would make her the envy of everyone in town. They were all clamoring for an audience with the strange little man.

Joyce was wearing her nicest dress, and forced her husband to wear his best suit. She'd had to force him to go out, period—he didn't like Capote. Harold snorted that Capote had already had his night on the town, then proceeded to tell his wife how he'd walked in on the writer in his hotel room and found him wearing a negligee. Joyce insisted her husband wouldn't know a negligee from a nighthawk, not having bought her one anytime recently, but Harold said, "No, Mother, I beg to differ," and described something silky and loose-fitting. It sure sounded like a negligee. Maybe it's what the fashionable people in New York were wearing these days, she told him, more to save the evening than anything else; she was willing to give Capote the benefit of the doubt. Harold wasn't willing to give Capote the benefit of anything, but he went along for the sake of his wife.

She was going to get a nice dinner out of her husband's job—he'd missed plenty of dinners because of it, that's for sure—and some stories for the girls at the club, maybe even an interview by the society editor of the *Garden City Gazette*. Maybe she could even write up the story herself, get Nelle Harper to help her put it together. They could be friends; as small-town as Joyce was, playing the piano at church, the go-to lady who put the crackers and Kool-Aid together for communion, Nelle had never made her feel like she was just being used to get a good story about the Clutters.

Joyce's only disappointment about the night was that the weather was so bad outside, she'd have to mess up the whole effect of her nice dress by putting her ugly gray coat on over it.

Oh, well, life in the plains, where the cold winds blew through everything in their path.

—

Back at the Muehlebach Hotel—the only choice in Kansas City for visiting dignitaries and famous writers like himself—Truman knocked on the door that separated his room from Nelle's. She answered, a reluctant debutante, dressed for her night on the town in her best black suit.

Truman gave her the once-over.

"You're not wearin' that, are you? Looks like you're dressed for a funeral."

"And you're not wearin' *that*, are you? Looks like *you're* dressed for *The World of Suzie Wong*."

He was wearing a negligee, no other word for it.

It was a drapey silk kimono thing, and in all the nights they'd gathered to write up their notes, she'd never seen it. Turquoise and pink and silver, with little geishas crossing bridges and serving tea, and doing things the Kama Sutra only hinted at.

"Better change. We're here to *write* about murder, not *get* murdered."

"You'd have the suit to be buried in if we do."

"You said wear something nice; this is the nicest thing I have."

"You need color. This whole drab town needs color. If I wasn't so exhausted from researchin' this damn book, I'd buy a few buckets of red paint and splash 'em everywhere."

"I s'pose that explains your getup."

"Laugh, you dreary people, laugh, but what will you do for fun when I'm gone?"

Truman's eyes went almost dead when he said it, as if he very much knew what was being said about him, as if he had already practiced his good-bye speech, long before he'd made his good-byes.

For a second Nelle felt sorry for him, but then the light seemed to come back into his eyes and he grabbed her by her freckled wrist, pulling her into his suite as he kept talking.

"I am most certainly *not* wearin' this. Number one, it's not warm enough, and number two, it's more than these people deserve. I'll give these people what they deserve . . ."

"Truman, what do you have up that danglin' kimono sleeve of yours?"

"Nothin'. Just a night away from murder, like you're cravin'. I've already called ahead and had the sommelier put his finest champagne on reserve; his only champagne, I think, the one and only bottle in the entire fruited plains. It should be appropriately chilled by the time we get there, just like moi."

Still pulling Nelle by the wrist, Truman marched to an open trunk in his room and pulled the perfect scarf from it, a flash of color like a bouquet of bright flowers from underneath a magician's dull handkerchief. He whipped it around her neck so fast she got whiplash.

"There, the corpse gets accessorized."

He then shook the kimono from his shoulders, a perfectly timed shimmy, and the whole thing slid off to reveal a natty little wool suit underneath, with red pinstripes, and a bow tie.

"Now we're ready for a night you'll never forget . . ."

—

Outside the hotel, their driver waited behind the wheel: Ray Cosgrove, a teenage bellhop from the hotel, with acne, glasses, and his hair pomaded into a peak, not that different from Kenyon Clutter. In place of the hotel uniform they usually saw him in—which made him look like one of the flying monkeys from The Wizard of Oz—he even wore a letter jacket.

Ray would remain Truman's chauffeur of choice during his many trips to Kansas; on Truman's very last trip there, Ray would drive him back from the prison in a pelting rain, just after he'd witnessed Dick and Perry hang. Truman would cry all the way; by then, Ray had learned not to say a word. At the end of his career, decades later, Ray would be in charge of the Muehlebach's bellhops, still wearing the same uniforms.

But this was just the start of their relationship: Truman waved a fifty under Ray's nose, and said its twin would be waiting on the other side of the witching hour of midnight if Ray would stay on call the entire night.

Before Nelle could say, "Midnight? How long does dinner . . ." Truman had moved on.

"Raymond, d'you know Nelly 'n me, we're married?"

Ray was young; it was 1961, but he wasn't dumb. In the rearview mirror, Nelle saw his face shape into a question mark.

Her face would have, too, had she not remembered the quickie marriage so vividly. Truman had been seven, she six; a child bride, to say the least. Her brother Ed had officiated, and Truman had volunteered Sook and Old John from his side of the family to serve as best man and woman. Sook had performed refreshment duty, making a cake with royal frosting, and Nelle had dragged her mother's wedding dress and veil out of the attic. That was another reason they had to get it done in a hurry; Lord help her if Amasa had come home and found her traipsing through the red Alabama dirt in her mother's wedding dress. But surprisingly, her mother thought it was cute; she even played "The Twelfth of Never" and "Ave Maria" on the piano for the young couple. Never mind that it was something of a shotgun wedding—Nelle being the one who held her BB gun on Truman and forced him to marry her, just an hour or so before his relatives took him to the train station to go back north for the fall.

Truman had slipped a paper band from the cigars his new step-
father manufactured on her ring finger, and she said she would
wear it always. She did, until her next good bath soaked it off,
and the bits of shiny colored paper floated down the drain.

"Yep, had to marry her before the baby was born." Truman let
loose with a high-pitched cackle.

"Step on it!"

Either in fear, shock, or disgust, Ray did, and they lurched into
the snow and the night.

—

In the darkness of the backseat:

"You still love me, Nellybelle?"

"'Course I do, long as you keep the checks comin' from Mr.
Shawn."

"No, I mean it. D'you love me? D'you know I'd never hurt you?"

For all his frivolity earlier in the evening—how seriously could
she take a man in a kimono?—he seemed deadly serious now. But
she couldn't answer him in kind.

"'Course I do. 'I do.' That's what I said under our tree when I
was six, and I repeat it now."

But Truman wouldn't take her joking. All this looking and
thinking on death must have set him on a different path; she'd
never seen him so solemn, as he looked at her with those same
ancient eyes she'd known since childhood. Eyes that now looked
hurt, or scared, or already apologetic.

She slapped his hand.

"Truman, stop it, you're spookin' me. I put on the nicest getup
I have; what else do you want?"

Truman was silent.

He was getting stranger and stranger, and they left Ray thinking the same thing, as he drove them just a block and a half away to The Grill, between Thirty-fifth and Thirty-sixth streets. They could have walked it, even in the snow and slush, but Truman announced that people didn't walk to a night on the town.

The restaurant was the only building on the downtown block that still had its lights on, glowing through the vaporous cold. It was beautiful; it could have been Victorian London instead of Kansas. Maybe it was going to be a nice night after all, when Nelle could sit back and forget about murder.

—

Outside, in the front seat of the car he had borrowed from his parents, Ray Cosgrove snuggled deeper in his letter jacket, wrapped his arms around himself, and took a swig from the apple brandy Mr. Truman had slipped him earlier in the evening.

It was the most exciting night of his life.

—

As Truman stepped inside the nicest restaurant in town, he felt a chemical change take place on his face—the roasting cold of the outside meeting the cozy warmth of the inside, where a fireplace blazed. At the exact spot high on his cheekbones where the two temperatures met, one of the few places on his body uncovered at that moment, Truman's skin felt red hot and roaring-white cold at the exact same time, almost canceling each other out, but each tingling and fighting for dominance. He stood still, trying to sear the exact sensation into his memory, and into words. It was the description he had been looking for all day, the exact feeling the Clutters must have experienced when the scorching heat of the bullets had entered the paralyzed cold of their flesh:

Fire meets ice.

There it was.

He was glad he had come, thinking a night off had already served what a full day of questions and grim photographs had not been able to accomplish.

And then he returned to more mundane matters, and worried whether he had ruined his shoes in the snow. Oh, well, it didn't matter; now he knew what it felt like to get shot to death.

Even Nelle, who could give a tinker's damn about her shoes, was already thinking ahead to how she'd get the circle of crusty salt and ice off them in the morning.

But there was no time for either of them to dwell on their shoes, because the Nyes were already standing up at their table and waving them in.

Truman plonked himself down and said to the waiter, "I'll have a stiff one, and then I'll have a drink."

The Nyes didn't laugh.

They didn't get it.

Under the table, Nelle slapped Truman on the knee and gave him a look that said, *Behave yourself.*

She got it.

That's the kind of evening it was going to be.

With a crook of his forefinger, Truman signaled for the champagne; Joyce, who rarely had champagne, sneezed when she sniffed the bubbles, and thought, "Now I'm drunk. There goes my chance at the society column."

Nelle came to her defense.

"You don't have to drink it if you don't want to; I'm sure Truman'll lap up whatever goes untouched."

"No, I'm gonna be a good boy tonight. Nelle Harper has had it with me and said she's gonna pack up her bags if I don't give her a night off from murder. So that subject is verboten."

He paused dramatically, as only he could do, his voice, eyebrows, everything at a high pitch that left a question dangling in the air.

"But then what the hell *are* we gonna talk about?"

That broke the ice, and they all laughed, even churchgoing Joyce, and clinked their glasses.

Two hours later, after Chateaubriand, which Truman ordered for them all—rare and don't think about cooking it a second longer, he wanted it bloody, it was the only way to eat good meat—all they had talked about was the murder, and Nelle Harper had forgotten about wanting nothing to do with it. Harold Nye had become as mesmerizing a storyteller as Truman could be, telling them how he had gone to Mexico to retrieve the radio and binoculars the killers had stolen from the Clutters' house, how he had searched from pawn shop to pawn shop to find them, how he had to pull over to the side of the road when he finally had them in hand, thinking about what had gone on in that house, and how the Clutters had once held these things.

He had never even told his wife that; Truman drew it out of him. Joyce was amazed; this was a man who barely grunted yes or no. She was so proud of him; he was the best husband in the world, and Truman and Nelle would be their best new friends now.

She didn't want the night to end.

For dessert, Truman ordered baked Alaska, the house specialty;

the owner himself wheeled it out on a cart, the browned peaks of meringue as beckoning as the warm glow of lights inside the frosty windows had been when they first arrived. He struck a long-handled match and prepared to light it, but Truman held up his hand to halt the action: he took the match by the stem and presented it to Harold Nye, payment for a good story, another morsel for his book.

Harold, who had never lit a dessert in his life and wasn't about to start now—or eaten a dessert that was on fire, for that matter—passed the match on to Joyce, an Olympic relay runner passing the torch. She giggled—that champagne had gone down easily, after the first few sips—and blessed the frosty icing with the gift of fire.

The flames whooshed into being, beautiful blue and orange and yellow and even green, and they all pulled back, then clapped—even Truman, the magician behind the trick, who knew it never failed to deliver.

When the owner moved back in to cut the loaf, Truman shooed him away again. He took the knife himself and made the first cut; the blade went in so easily, a clean slice through the white peaks, then stopped when it hit the frozen brick of Neapolitan ice cream underneath. Soft, hard, ease, resistance, then give: Truman kept pushing until the knife went all the way in, stopping only when it hit the glass plate at the very bottom.

Fire and ice indeed.

This night was a blessing, and it was just starting.

Oh, this night was young, and cold; there were places to see, and miles to go, before they slept.

Truman teased his companions by letting them have a few bites of the frozen dessert before he threw a handful of bills, crisp and fresh from the bank, on the table, so close to the candle they almost went up in flames. In the breeze, the candle sputtered, just as the diners did, their forks in midair.

They weren't finished.

Never mind; Truman was, or rather, he was just beginning, as he flung his scarf around his neck and it, too, almost caught the flame. Only Harold's quick reflexes kept Truman from setting himself on fire, as he grabbed the fringed edges of the scarf and tamped them out on the table. Truman barely realized he'd just been saved, as he dragged them out of the restaurant, half in and half out of their coats, the scent of scorched wool trailing behind them.

Outside, Truman insisted on taking a picture to commemorate the night, and hauled Ray out of the waiting car to snap it.

"Say cheese!"

"Say freeze!"

The flash went off, freezing the four in a different way, for posterity. In a spontaneous moment, fueled by the champagne, they linked arms—Nelle, Harold, Joyce, and Truman.

Truman began herding them into the back of the car, as Harold tried to resist.

"But we're parked down there . . ."

"You didn't think this was it, did you? Oh, no, sir, we're just gettin' started. The night is young, and so are we . . ."

The car was filled with the heady, thick aroma of grease and fried chicken and apple brandy, which Ray Cosgrove had dined on in their absence; it didn't mix with Chateaubriand and champagne and baked Alaska. Joyce was trying to remember the taste of the flavors for her article, moving her tongue around in her mouth to lock them there, afraid the other smells would make her forget. For some reason, she gripped her husband's hand tighter.

Truman slid into the front seat, next to Ray.

"Lake and High, and make it snappy."

It wasn't a neighborhood nice people went to.

"You sure you have that right?"

"You sure you want that other fifty?"

It was the end of the discussion, a question with a question.

Nelle shifted around to press her face into the cool, sweaty damp of the back window; she needed the cold against her skin to wake her up, for whatever was in store. Somehow, she knew they were leaving something behind, and she wanted to look at it one last time, before everything changed.

—

They stood outside what looked like a warehouse, on the outskirts of town; the street was paved with bricks. (And the road to hell . . . never mind.) There was a single door and no sign.

They all stood outside the car, stamping their feet to try to stay warm.

"Stay here."

Truman threw open the door and marched up a narrow stair-case, to the light of a single unshielded bulb at the top landing.

"The dark at the top of the stairs," Truman said ominously, then giggled.

"No, see, there's a light up there," Harold responded, and Truman's giggle turned into a drunken roar.

"Oh, it's darker than you can imagine."

"Truman?"

It was a command, not a question, from Nelle.

His response was in kind.

"Nelle?"

She wanted back in the car, back to the smells of Ray's home-cooked supper. She wanted back in a tree in Monroeville, back in a walk-up flat in Manhattan, back anywhere except here.

Something wasn't right.

At the top of the stairs, Truman flicked off bills from a seemingly infinite roll.

"One, two, three, four, five."

Money was the only way they were getting in, wherever they were.

Truman motioned for the others to come up. Joyce turned back to her husband; in silence, her face asked the question, "Do I dare?"

Harold turned to Nelle. "What's your little friend up to?"

"Buyin' the keys to the city? I don't know."

And she didn't. But they went up anyway.

At the top, a big man beckoned them inside.

"Right this way, Mr. Capote, ladies." Then, seeing Harold, he added, "Sir. Welcome to the Jewel Box."

He opened the door to a smoky haze; the lights were very low, but they could see men and women dancing. Joyce was the first to get excited.

"Oh, look, Hally, dancing! We haven't been dancing in years!"

Truman encouraged them.

"Yeah, 'Hally,' shake a leg."

"Need another drink for that, need to get my land legs before I shake 'em."

"Bet you could get a *really* stiff one here."

That was Truman, of course.

"Truman, I don't like this . . ."

That was Nelle.

"Oh, but you will, you will, just give it time . . ."

As Harold walked toward the bar, he accidentally bumped into a woman whose drink splashed.

"Oh, excu . . . Jesus."

The woman he had just knocked into was a man.

In a dress.

"Jesus Mary and Joseph . . ."

"I think you took a wrong turn on Mill Street, honey," the man/woman said, as he/she squeezed Harold's bicep through the shiny cloth of his jacket. He/she wafted away into the blackness of the room, as Harold thought all the cleaning in the world would never get the taint out of his favorite suit. He'd never be able to wear it again.

He grabbed his wife's hand and started to pull her toward the door, but Truman materialized to block their way.

"Don't rush, we just got here. At least stay until you take the chill off. I personally find it very warm and invitin' in here. And the stage show hasn't even started."

"Capote, you little pansy, my wife is a good Christian woman, and I'm a good Christian man, and if you think you're ever gonna get any more information out of me after a stunt like this . . . how dare you bring us to a place like this."

Harold wondered if he could arrest them all, starting with Truman. He was, after all, an officer of the law, but he didn't want to touch them, let alone arrest them.

Men whose eyes looked frozen in headlights.

Men whose eyes were ringed with mascara.

Men with Brylcreemed hair, and bouffants, and Christmas sweaters tucked into slacks, and rep ties like English schoolboys, and someone who looked like Perry Como . . .

Men.

But nobody else like Truman.

"You gave me a story about Dick and Perry, I wanted to give you one about them . . . and this is it. This is what was going on in their heads, men with men, just like it was in prison. They were lovers, haven't you figured that out yet?"

He practically screamed it, but the decibels were lost in the din of the place.

Joyce, terrified of looking small-town in the face of Truman, and already calculating if she should include this visit in her article, said, "Well, it's very . . ."

"Interesting? Is that the word you were going to use? Interestin'? It's not interesting, it's sick."

In that moment, Truman sounded as if he hated himself, not for what he was, but for what he had just done.

By then, some of the patrons realized who Truman was. They flocked to him, plying him with questions and flattery, playing with his ears. At least that's what it looked like to Harold, more ammunition that it was sick. Who'd play with somebody's ears? Freak show. They grabbed Truman's scarf and turned it into a maypole game, skipping around him and draping it around his neck. Someone pulled it off and, in a sleight of hand worthy of Houdini, exchanged it for a feather boa.

Harold wanted them to keep going.

"Wrap it around his scrawny neck till he chokes."

Nelle spoke up, the smoke from so many cigarettes burning her eyes—and she was a smoker.

"Truman Streckfus Persons"—for that was the real name he was born with—"you've pulled some wild stunts in your life, but this wasn't called for, so we're goin'. You can stay if you want, but you'll have to walk, 'cause *we're* takin' that car out there your good friend Ray has waitin' by . . ."

And they all three walked out, leaving Truman standing under a smoky spotlight, with a ragged pink boa wrapped around his neck.

But when Truman walked downstairs minutes later, he found Nelle waiting for him. The car was gone, the Nyes were gone, and she was alone.

She couldn't tell Truman why she had waited, and he didn't ask; just took her by the hand, as he had done since they were five years old, and pulled her alongside him to another lone door in the wintry landscape.

"Looks like it's just us, Nellybelle. Guess we've had this date from the beginnin' . . ."

The sound he made was something between a cackle and a cry, but she didn't stop him. She couldn't move on her own anymore; she could barely think as he opened the next door and led her in.

—

He had never told her he was homosexual, but she knew. At six years old, she knew that this delicate, ancient creature living next to her was something very fine and rare and different. They grew up, they moved apart, she heard what people whispered about him, but he had never said it aloud to her, so it didn't exist.

Nobody knew who she was, so there were no whispers about her, except the whispers she made to herself late at night.

Now, it was as if Truman had heard those whispers, whispers that had become prayers, and brought her to the place where they could be answered. It was the place where she could finally say them aloud, but she had lost her voice, and Truman had to speak for her.

"Here, drink me . . ."

It was the note that had greeted Alice, in Wonderland, the drink that had made Alice only ten inches tall.

That's what Nelle wanted to be, the smallest woman in the room, instead of the Paul Bunyan lumberjack, the tree trunk, she was. She wanted to be so small she could disappear, but still be there, so drink it she did, and when Truman said drink some more, she did that, too, and it felt good, and she wanted to pour an entire bottle of burning liquid down her throat to fan the flames and put out the fire at the same time.

"I've seen fire and I've seen ice . . ."

Nonsense phrases were forming in her head, as her brain shut down and lines from a beloved Robert Frost poem channeled through her body to her mouth and tongue and teeth and lips, and she said it aloud to no one, and everyone . . .

". . . and some say the world shall end by fire, but I think by ice, and . . . something something desire, but that would be nice . . ."

She was babbling, words she knew by heart but could no longer remember.

Fire and ice; now she knew what it felt like to be shot, just as Truman did.

She knew what it felt like to be the Clutters.

Truman looked at her as if he were welcoming her into a very exclusive club, watched her as she couldn't meet his gaze but turned her eyes to the other women in the room instead.

Women who looked like men.

Women who looked like they belonged to a third sex that

hadn't yet been named, with skin tanned from sports and hair cut so short you could see scalp underneath it.

Women who were more beautiful than any of the starlets Truman had ever collected for his scrapbooks, their skin so white they must have bathed in cream, their hair so shiny and silken and blond it was like the hair angels must have.

And now Nelle whispered, her first words to Truman that weren't a poem.

"Why did you have to go and ruin it all?"

"So your prayers can be answered, little sister, just like mine."

Nelle's voice got a little louder.

"I help you, I follow you, I pick up the pearls you drop, I get you into these people's house . . ."

". . . and I got you into this house. It's the one you've been wanting to visit most of all, isn't it? Your own key to unlock the door . . . and all it takes is saying yes, yes . . . whisper it if you have to . . ."

But she couldn't say it.

All she could do was run out of the house into the burning cold, leaving her footprints behind in the snow.

She ran and ran and didn't quit running until she got back to her hotel, slipping and sliding in the ice, no thought of a salt-ring buildup on her shoes now.

And where did Truman run to, that little boy/man who had told her just hours ago he would never hurt her, who had written about outcasts adrift in a giant tree, telling soul secrets late into the night? Where was the ancient little boy who had worshipped a wounded and backward old woman named Sook, who went deep into childhood forests with her to pick windfall pecans and bargain with Indians for moonshine? Where was the little boy who went to the pictures every Saturday, with the nickel he had hoarded during the week, then came home and acted out his version of the movie, better than Hollywood's? When had that little boy turned into a monster, still standing in the slush at the corner of Thirty-fifth and Thirty-sixth streets of a strange city?

That little boy was long gone, if he had ever existed in the first place. Maybe he had always been a fiction, and Nelle had been as suckered in by him as the next ticket buyer; he lived only in print, a towheaded changeling child who had to drain the life from others before he could take form and shape himself.

A vampire who lived on ink instead of blood.

Nelle felt the kind of rage at Truman that could cause someone to pull a trigger four times, as Perry had done inside the Clutters' house.

She was so mad she could pull the trigger five times, with the revolver Truman had asked her to buy. She found herself holding it, even though she didn't remember picking it up. Alone in her Kansas hotel room, she knew how a gun must have made those killers feel, like no one could hurt them anymore. She wanted to shoot it, shoot away her pain and confusion; she wanted to witness destruction.

She moved to the door that adjoined her room with Truman's and gripped the doorknob. It would be a contest: whichever thing she squeezed harder—the doorknob or the gun's trigger—would be the winner.

She would rather have squeezed out tears, to get the poison of what Truman had forced her to confront out of her system. But tears wouldn't come; she was too mad for tears. Pain did come, though; she squeezed so hard into the ornate filigree design on the doorknob that it bit into her flesh, leaving a red welt.

She squeezed harder; she wanted blood.

She saw the veins distend out on both wrists.

By the grace of God, by a hair, she squeezed the doorknob tighter than the gun.

It swung open, and she was in Truman's room: the Underwood typewriter, the liquor bottles, the kimono with butterfly-shaped sleeves, the piles and piles of notes they had made in black-and-white journals.

She wanted to rip it all up, splatter cartridge pen ink over everything, take it all away, just as he had taken everything away from her.

On the bedside table was a single copy of Other Voices, Other Rooms, propped up on a reading stand as if it were the bejeweled Gutenberg Bible. She picked the book up and saw him in his author's photo, lounging on a divan and looking doe-eyed, staring back at her from the back cover.

If the author wasn't here for her to shoot, she'd shoot his photo instead.

But she couldn't shoot a book, or a gun, any more than she could kill a mockingbird.

She had to do something to relieve the pain.

She picked up the book and smashed it—face-first—into an ornate mirror in the room.

A crack, then a thunk, as the book stopped dead in the thick wood behind the beveled glass. In the splinters and prisms, she could still see the photo of Truman.

She could also see herself.

And she had no clue which one she was really aiming at.

She ran out of the room and didn't stop running until she was back in New York, and even there, she kept running, until she'd finally run all the way back home, to Monroeville.

—

But her footprints were still out there in Kansas, frozen in time; she saw them, as she stared at the photograph in her hands. A photograph someone had sent her, nearly twenty-five years after the longest night of her life.

Fire and ice.

She shivered and couldn't stop shaking, just like the people in the picture.

Chapter Fourteen

As soon as Myrtle opened the door in the morning, first thing Truman did was announce they were having a party.

A big one.

"My book's back, and I'm putting it in hiding. Nobody will ever find it now, till I'm ready for them to. Danny's gone, and he's never coming back, so we have to celebrate. Another party. Bigger than the first. No more black and white. Color."

Myrtle was used to his pronouncements, and usually didn't pay much attention to them. She said words just to fill up the air, on her way to the kitchen to get her first cup of coffee of the day. "Long as I don't have to cook for it . . . don't wanna wear no fancy shoes neither . . . long as you can guarantee me them two things . . ."

"If you don't show a little more excitement, I might not invite you at all. Maybe I will, maybe I won't. I've been up all night planning it."

He grabbed her by her uncaffeinated arm and pulled her into his inner sanctum, where the "plan" was revealed in a single image. Photos and pictures from his files, the ones he usually reserved for his snake boxes and kites, were flung all over the room, but a new, lone picture, torn from the fancy art book of one of his friends, adorned a central place over his desk on the wall—the very spot Myrtle had rubbed bare trying to get the snake off it.

"There. That's the theme. Whaddaya think?"

"A big mess with a little bit of snake? That's what your party's about? Ain't gonna do no cleanin', neither . . ."

"There."

He literally put his hands on either side of her head and positioned her eyes in line with the picture:

"*There.* The Arabian Nights."

It was a glossy print of an Arabian palace: columns draped in gauzy, jewel-colored curtains, brass bottles with incense wafting out of them, and a snake charmer in the corner, the flute at his lips enticing a snake out of a basket.

"That's it! That's me!"

Myrtle didn't know if he was talking about the charmer, or the snake.

He read her mind.

"The man. I'm the snake charmer! That's gonna be my costume. I'll be in the corner, all in white, but rags. White rags. I'll hobble in disguised as a beggar, which is what I've always been, picking at scraps from their tables. They won't know it's me, they'll treat me like dirt until the stroke of midnight, when I remove my disguise, then they'll all be revealed for the shams they are. The men in black caftans, the women in veils, everybody takes off their disguises at midnight. I'll have incense and smoke everywhere, like a Turkish bazaar, and I'll have storytelling booths, and people telling fantastic yarns, like Scheherazade . . ."

"Shehera who?"

"She had to tell stories to save her life, and if her stories weren't good enough, they'd kill her—just like me. She could have been my twin sister. I had to worm my way into their courts, but if I wasn't amusing enough, they'd cast me out, so believe me, I've sung for my table scraps plenty, and now, they'll be singing for theirs . . . and if they want anything other than gruel to eat, they'll have to kiss the snake charmer's hand, but I'll cover it with warts. They'll be beggin' to come anyway. At midnight, I'll take the silver covers off their plates, and everybody'll have one of my new books sittin' there instead of food. Then they can read what fools they are, treatin' me like a beggar. They'll see who the beggar really is. It'll be bigger than the party in '66. That one had five hundred and forty . . . this one'll have a thousand. I'm gonna start working on an invitation list right now . . ."

He'd barely paused to take a breath.

He was high as one of his kites, flying on something.

He plunked down on the couch with a fresh journal, and the pages of the new book that had been returned to him. He wet a pencil lead with the tip of his tongue and started writing, but his revenge fantasy must have worn him out. By the time Myrtle came out of the kitchen with her coffee, Truman was asleep, Maggie the bulldog curled up and drooling next to him. They looked so peaceful Myrtle felt like sliding in next to them for warmth and comfort, molding her knees behind the fold of Truman's, throwing her big arms around his even bigger belly, to become a big tangle of fat. A big black and white spoon, that's what it would be. It wouldn't be romantic, just peaceful, after the stress of her mission to the post office—and the other thing. But no, she couldn't mess up that spoon, man and dog; they were perfect together.

Truman snorted, and the pages on his chest shook.

Maggie pawed at them in her sleep, chasing a rabbit: a quiver, then deep panting, her front legs and back jerking as if all four were attached to electrodes. Now Truman's legs started quivering, too, in sympathy: chasing something, or running from it?

Myrtle was tempted to snatch the book from him—she'd be doing him a favor, in case he let go and all those pages scattered over the floor, or Maggie slobbered on them and the words all ran together, but she knew she'd be violating a trust. From all the fuss he put up, it was clear he didn't want anybody reading this book, not yet.

She'd let him keep his book "top secret!" but she couldn't resist looking at the notebook in which he had begun his party plans. Her head bobbed up and down as she tried to keep pace with his rising and falling chest; the notebook rose and fell along with it, but she was able to see the one and only page he had completed before sleep and party dreams took over.

On one column he had written *To Invite*: the one and only name, so far, was hers: Myrtle J. Bennett.

On another column he'd written *To Keep Out at Any Cost*: Danny.

Next to his name, a question mark.

So much for casting him out forever.

Revenge must be exhausting, but good for the soul, Myrtle decided; Truman's face looked tired, but peaceful. She thought she should try some revenge; she needed some peace right now. It was only when Truman was asleep that Myrtle could see it, only when slumber and dreams allowed his face to relax enough to allow some sweetness to come through, that Myrtle saw what he must have been like as a child. The bags and broken capillaries and wrinkles and nastiness fell away, and his skin became smooth and unblemished again. She wasn't a stupid woman; she knew everybody else looked at Truman and saw only what he'd become: bloated, drugged out, cruel. He was cruel so often, she doubted he even knew the difference between cruelty and kindness anymore. But no, she saw something else. Sleeping, he could have been six years old, tender and innocent and sad.

He was her baby, and babies were supposed to be tender and innocent, but not sad.

Sad, no little child deserved that.

It wasn't fair.

It wasn't right.

Out of nowhere, tears started running down her cheeks.

She wasn't crying for Truman.

She was crying for herself.

She wouldn't make it long enough to go to his party, unless he had it tomorrow.

She was going to die.

They'd gotten it all wrong.

Truman's ghosts were coming for her.

Those folks she'd never met, Nancy and Kenyon and Perry—they were her harbingers, not Truman's.

They were paving the way for her.

She had cancer, and she didn't have much time left.

Who was going to take care of her sleeping Truman now?

She'd found out over the weekend, when she'd lied to Truman and told him her husband was taking her away for a second honeymoon—second honeymoon, humph, thirty years too late. Said he was gonna take her to Vegas to play some craps; Truman gave her a hundred dollars and said throw some for me. She hadn't liked lying to him, but she didn't want Truman to know she was going to the doctor. She had a bad feeling about all the blood and weight she'd been losing lately.

Her bad feeling was right.

When she'd gone back to the doctor a few days later for the results, after delivering that package at the post office, she'd taken one look at the doc's face and said, "Don't even bother telling me, I don't wanna put you through it. It's not your bad news, it's mine." If there was anything Truman had taught her, it was how to read the look on somebody's face. In her mind, it was a better thing to read than some old book.

Right now, she was mostly worried about how—or if—she was gonna break the news to Truman, and who she was gonna get to take care of him, after she was gone. She couldn't go to her grave in peace if she didn't have that figured out. Maybe that Joanne Carson, Johnny's ex-wife; she called Truman all the time, about the only person who did call anymore. Or maybe that Nelle woman, that Truman was sending his boxes to. Maybe Myrtle could make up a really giant box and ship Truman off to her in that, with a note pinned to his shirt.

Or maybe the good Lord would take Truman first and she wouldn't have to worry; the way he—Truman, not the good Lord—was going, it wouldn't surprise her. One day, she'd gotten so mad she'd scooped up all his pills and thrown 'em in the pool—all those brown and orange see-through bottles, just floating along the top. But she knew she wasn't doing it for real; Truman called it an "empty, symbolic gesture." If she'd really meant business, he said, she would have unscrewed the lids and dumped the pills in, bottle by bottle, so the pills would dissolve in the water. When he told her that, she realized it was true. He'd already won. She used the fishnet pole to scoop out the bottles, along with a handful of waterlogged leaves and a tadpole.

Truman took the bottles out of the soggy net one at a time, read their labels, dried them off, and kissed them. Then he solemnly kissed Myrtle, too—"I thank you for trying"—before he returned them all to his hidey-holes in the house.

Just before he went inside, he turned around and said, "Sometimes symbolic gestures are all we have left."

She wasn't sure what it meant, but she knew it made her sad.

Even sadder: sometimes he'd beg her to hide the pills from him, and five minutes later, now with tears in his eyes, beg her to tell him where they were. She'd give in, with tears in her eyes, too, and know she was killing him.

And sadder still: here she was about to meet her Maker, and it was Truman she was worried about.

She knew she'd lived a good life, wasn't any confusion about that. When she stood before the good Lord for her final review—other than Him saying she should have lost a few pounds—he'd have to nod His head and agree she'd done her best. Even trying to blow up Mr. Danny's car, she'd done that to make Truman happy.

But other than kindness, what did she have to show for her life? You'd go in Truman's house, see his books lined up in all sorts of languages on the shelves, so many he hadn't even broken the covers of most of them. Did she have a shelf full of books to show? No, just a clothesline full of maid's uniforms, blowing in the breeze. But wasn't that something? The smell of freshness they gave off, their cool damp to the touch; she'd seen Truman go running through the clothesline, letting the wet uniforms slap against his face. She knew that didn't make him a pervert, sniffing some maid's uniforms. He always came back in talking about his childhood after he'd done that, how that was something he used to do in Alabama, how happy that made him. Wet wash on the line, the best perfume in the world, he called it. Maybe they could market it.

That was something you could put on a tombstone, wasn't it, that you'd made somebody happy, if just for a moment?

Damn it.

How was she going to tell Truman?

She was going to call that Nelle woman right now, while Truman was asleep. She'd put her thoughts right out there, and get her to take over.

And while she had her on the phone, she'd apologize for sending that box full of snake guts.

Just then, Maggie snored and liked to scare her to death, a bit too early, and Truman started moaning in his sleep.

"No, no, get away . . . I will not apologize . . ."

Guess they both had ghosts coming to take them away.

Chapter Fifteen

Truman had taught Nelle well, a lesson from the old masters: when a gun got introduced into a story, it had to go off.

She just didn't know when yet.

But she knew it would.

Listen to her, Wyatt Earp, quivering in her bed with a gun in her hand. She'd do better with a golf club.

It was the first time she'd held it since nearly twenty-five years ago, that last night in Truman's hotel room. After looking at that picture of the four of them in the snow, she'd retrieved it from the bottom of the file cabinet where she kept her letters to Ed. She'd kept it there all those years since Kansas, untouched and unfired. She gripped it even tighter now, wishing she had waited for Truman in his room back then, instead of smashing his mirror and running away to New York.

She'd started out this night with the gun under her pillow; she didn't know where else to put it, now that it was back in her life. (Wasn't there some old wives' tale in the back of her head, literally: sleep with a gun under your pillow and you'll dream about . . . ?) She didn't want to hold it all night long—that was surely an invitation for it to go off—but she didn't want to just leave it lying loose on top of the bedcovers, either. She'd have one stray muscle twitch in the middle of the night and bam, there goes a big toe, or worse. So she'd removed it from underneath the pillow, not wanting whatever kind of dream it might presage.

Too late.

She was holding the gun in both hands, its nose pointing toward the door, when Bonnie Clutter timidly stuck her head into the room.

It's hard to tell who was more scared: Nelle, at seeing another ghost, or Bonnie, at seeing another gun pointed at her, when it was the last thing she'd seen on earth. They both reacted at exactly the same time: Nelle yelled "Sweet Jesus" and dropped the gun, and Bonnie saw a tiny spark of flame come ripping out of the barrel, a replay of the single gunshot that had ended her life.

The bullet lodged in the doorjamb, and Bonnie Clutter vanished, to be replaced by someone else, in the flesh.

Alice.

Awakened from her sleep.

There was no mistaking her for a timid ghost.

Even in the middle of the night, minus her tennis shoes and hearing aid, she was a formidable presence. Nelle wasn't sure she wouldn't rather deal with a ghost.

"SweetJesusLord," Alice said, taking in her sister, who had now picked up the gun. It was pointing at her.

Probably by accident.

"Since when did you start packing heat when you went to sleep?"

"It went off. It's the gun I've had since Kansas. I got it out of the office tonight."

"Why." When Alice asked a question, it didn't have a question mark at the end of it.

Nelle couldn't answer. She didn't know why she had brought the gun into her bedroom.

"Planning on doing me in? Let me remind you, little sis, you're the one with all the money. Not gonna get a penny out of me, dead or alive. I'll take this if you don't mind; need you around to make my breakfast in the A.M."

Alice retrieved the gun, holding it at arm's length as if it were a dirty diaper.

"I'm in court tomorrow, so I'd be beholden if you kept the activity in here to a minimum. And if you need the services of a gun, just yell out, and I'll come blazin'. Evidently, my hand's steadier than yours. And a pleasant good night to you, too."

Both sisters waited that extra second, as if they had secrets to tell each other and just needed a little opening to let them come pouring out: Nelle, of the other packages she'd now received; Alice, of snooping in her sister's office. But neither was going to make the first move.

After decades together, neither was going to make the first move. Alice left, a "You had your chance" in her eyes.

Nelle's eyes followed Alice's departing figure down the hall, and another shadowy form began taking her place. Whether it was Nelle's old eyelids drooping and forming spontaneous cataracts, or sleep coming back on much too fast, or the limbo land between dream and sleep, she didn't know. Wisp, air, form, veil, hat, suit— in a few seconds, the ephemera became Bonnie Clutter once more, peeping back in, deceased but undeterred, done up in a little hat with organza flowers covered by a net. It was as if she'd dressed up for a special occasion; the hat and veil all but managed to hide the gaping hole in the center of her forehead.

Nelle wasn't sure if Bonnie even knew she was dead.

"Mrs. Clutter?"

"Just call me Bonnie. Everybody does."

It was something Bonnie Clutter had rarely said in the living world, not because she was unduly formal, but because she was almost too shy to tell people to call her anything. It must have taken everything she had to pull herself together for this earthly visitation, and Nelle had almost ended it, at the wrong end of a gun that hadn't seen the light of day, or night, for twenty-five years.

Bonnie waited a moment, then timidly asked, but with pride, "My goodness, does everybody down here have a gun in the house now, for protection? Is that because of us?"

Since this was only the second ghost Nelle had ever welcomed into her bedroom in the middle of the night, she didn't know how to answer. But she didn't want to scare her off again.

Nelle held out her hands; they were empty.

"I'm so sorry, the gun, it's gone now, see . . . I got it when we went to Kansas, but . . . you're safe. It's gone now. My sister . . . she took the gun, although between us, I don't know which is scarier . . . my sister or a gun . . ."

She was rattling on as nervously as if she were at her first job interview.

Or like she'd never seen a ghost before.

Bonnie stuck her head a bit farther into the room, not completely taking Nelle's word for it. She lifted the veil from her hat and looked around the room suspiciously, as if someone else might be hiding in the corner.

"You'd think I'd be over it by now, but I'm not. The kids and Herb have moved on, but I . . ."

She stopped, shaking her head.

"It's not something you get over quickly."

Nelle didn't know what to say to that, so she stayed quiet, and let Bonnie find her way. Bonnie Clutter, the mother of Kenyon and Nancy, standing at the exact spot Kenyon had just nights ago. He had leaned insolently against the doorjamb, holding a cigarette; Bonnie leaned against the wall for support, as if she would collapse without it.

She was so tiny. Even after all the pictures Nelle had seen of her, and all the descriptions neighbors had given, Nelle wasn't prepared for how small she was. The little red suit she was wearing, it was so tiny it made Nelle want to cry. She couldn't imagine a big stern farm man like Herb Clutter with this little woman.

"This is my first trip . . . down here. Kenyon said I'd like it. He did, coming to visit you the other night. He said I'd like you, too. We don't have many secrets anymore, not like down here, but . . . we don't like to go where we're not welcome."

Bonnie Clutter was an apologetic woman, even in the afterlife.

Bonnie Clutter was a woman starved for company.

She ventured a little farther into the room now, touching things, as if remembering her room had been like this, too. They were both rooms without a man; Bonnie and Herb had slept in separate rooms for the last several years of their lives, Bonnie moving to the spare room on the second floor. Bonnie and Nelle both had antique furniture, a pretty mirror, doilies and lace, but not too much else, besides a Bible on the stand next to the bed. Bonnie seemed to like that. She smiled, as if thinking, *This is a good Christian woman. I can talk to her. She'll understand.* (Just as Nelle had once thought, when she was a visitor in Bonnie's bedroom, *I know this woman, I grew up with her, she could have been my mother.*)

Bonnie's fingers lingered on the Bible.

"'I lift mine eyes to the hills, from which cometh my help.' I said that, you know, that last night. But help . . . well, it never came. At least not the earthly kind . . ."

She shrugged her bony shoulders—her little knit suit, edged in black rickrack, rode up on them.

Bonnie Clutter was a woman who couldn't quite say what was on her mind, not yet.

But Nelle didn't want to rush her. She didn't want to wake up, if she was sleeping; she wanted to keep dreaming and find out what Bonnie Clutter was doing here.

She had questions for Bonnie, too.

But she had to start slow, so she started with a compliment.

"You raised a fine young man, that Kenyon. I sure did enjoy meeting him. I'm sure he makes you proud."

"Oh, that he does. Why, did you know, that boy was making a cedar chest down in the basement for his sister's wedding, his sister Beverly's wedding, and he'd just varnished it the very day those . . ."

She started shimmering, as if she were about to disappear again. The force of the word she couldn't say, and the image she didn't want to remember, were almost too much for her. But she marshaled on, as if her visit were part of some curative therapy plan.

". . . the very night those men came in, and that Perry . . ."

She spit the name out, her body wavering like a heat mirage in the desert.

Nelle interrupted. "You don't have to put yourself through this . . ."

"Yes, I do."

She took a deep breath, to steady herself.

"Yes, I do. That Perry put his knife down on the chest, and Kenyon, even tied up on the couch down in the basement, asked him to move it, because he didn't want it messing up the finish."

No mother had ever had to say such words about her son, words of such pride and anguish intermingled.

"Can you imagine a boy doing such a thing? With them standing right there, he's thinking about his sister's wedding . . ."

The memory had almost done Bonnie in, and she lurched toward the edge of Nelle's bed before she collapsed. Her eyelids were flickering, as if she were trying to remember the scene behind them—and bat it away at the same time.

She needed to remember it.

"They rigged those knots up so hard . . . you strained against them, it hurt even more . . . I hope he hurt. I hope Perry hurt when he died."

Bonnie's lips went white, they were clenched so tight.

Nelle could tell her Perry had hurt when he died, even though she hadn't been there to witness it. He'd asked her to be one of his witnesses, but she wouldn't dignify his death with that. He'd walked up the regulation thirteen steps, thirteen unlucky steps, to the gallows; a stranger, plucked from anonymity and paid in cash so there would be no record of his identity, put the noose over his head and pulled the trapdoor. He'd gone into freefall until he came to the end of the rope, then his heart kept beating for eighteen or nineteen minutes until he was pronounced dead.

Bonnie nodded her head in agreement, as if she could see the very things Nelle had just imagined.

"Good."

Nelle reached out to hold Bonnie's hand, to calm both of them down, and almost jerked it away when she felt how cold it was. But Bonnie held on fast.

"Why don't we go in the bathroom and wash your face," Nelle said, then remembered a bathroom was the last place Bonnie Clutter would want to go, having been pushed inside one and tied up in a chair there, as strangers rampaged through her house.

"Oh, good Lord, can't I just think for two seconds before I open my big fat mouth . . ."

"It's not the kind of thing you get over quickly," Bonnie said once again, shaking her head in remembrance.

Nelle's faux pas had her dying for a cigarette, but she knew it wasn't the right thing to do in front of Bonnie. But if not a cigarette, then maybe a cup of coffee; she needed something to steady her nerves. Maybe Bonnie would join her, the only one in the Clutter household who stood up to Herb's rule against spirits or stimulus.

As soon as she thought it, it was in their hands, two steaming mugs of piping hot coffee, with a little cream and sugar. Cups of coffee that appeared out of nowhere.

It was good against the shock of this nighttime visitation;

Bonnie removed her hand from Nelle to grip the cup with both hands, warming herself up. Nelle wondered if they had coffee in heaven, or even kitchens; did they even need to eat?

It was mostly all she thought about lately, what heaven would be like.

Bonnie seemed to hear her, without words.

"We have . . . whatever we need. Just . . . no dishes."

And she laughed, shyly, like someone who was testing the waters of a new vocabulary, wondering if she'd taken something in vain. The coffee mug shook in her hands and threatened to slosh over, but didn't.

"Don't know what I'd do without my coffee."

Bonnie took an extra-long draw from the cup and gargled it around in her mouth for warmth. Nelle saw it move around, as if she could see through the very skin of Bonnie's cheeks.

Was she dreaming?

Bonnie squeezed the mug tighter, and her birdlike hands pushed through its ceramic walls. The cup itself didn't move, but her hands transcended earthly physics and went directly into the hot liquid, without displacing a single drop or getting burned.

She didn't even notice what she had done.

Nelle was still looking at Bonnie's hands in shock when Bonnie started speaking, finally ready to get something off her chest.

"I wasn't a good mother to those kids. I was 'sickly,' that's the word everybody used, no use denying it, they certainly didn't mind telling it to you and Truman when you went asking around . . ."

She looked at Nelle, but somehow, it wasn't an accusation.

". . . but nobody could ever figure out what was wrong with me. I took to the bed, and Kenny and Nancy pretty much had to fend for themselves, not just on that last night, but . . ."

She started crying.

"Nancy could make a cherry pie like nobody's business. And Herb, he made coconut cookies that could've won a state fair prize. A man, mind you, a farmer, baking his own cookies, and had the idea of putting coconut in them. I barely ever made it to the kitchen."

Bonnie put the cup of coffee aside and touched her face to wipe away her tears. Nelle reached out to hold her hand again; this time, she felt how thin and arthritic it was, how prominent the veins were. Bonnie still wore her wedding ring; for some reason, the killers hadn't taken that, even though they'd looted the house for money. Herb had tried so hard to reassure his wife the men just wanted money and wouldn't hurt them. But that was the first wrong thing he had said to her that night, because Bonnie knew Herb didn't keep any money in the house.

It would just make the men madder.

Of all of them, she was the only one who knew how angry men got over money, and how the night would end.

A cold bathroom on a cold November night in Kansas.

Her husband nudged away with the tip of a long rifle.

The last glance that passed between them: Herb saying "Don't worry" with his eyes, Bonnie not even able to say "I love you" back with hers, because she was shaking so much.

Kenyon shoved down the stairs without his glasses.

Nancy practicing "Greensleeves" on her flute, that very night, but now she couldn't, because her hands were tied behind her back . . .

"STOP IT."

For a moment, Nelle wasn't sure which one of them had said it. Then she saw Bonnie looking at her askance, and realized the words had come out of her very own mouth, after seeing the same things Bonnie couldn't get out of her head.

"I'm sorry. I didn't mean to . . ."

Now words, not just pictures, came pouring out of Bonnie.

"Herb's not one to talk. He can barely tell ya what he wants for dinner, or if you cooked the steak too done. But if you don't let these things out, they'll just eat away . . . I don't have anybody to . . ."

She started crying even harder.

With those words, Nelle finally knew why Bonnie Clutter had come tonight: to have someone tell her to stop, that she didn't have to relive that night again and again, ever again.

Bonnie reached over and hugged Nelle around the shoulders.

Nelle could feel her.

This wasn't a dream.

"Oh, thank you."

It's like the stale old air stored up in Bonnie Clutter's lungs all these years could finally get released, now that the pictures were gone. She breathed in and out a few times, feeling how good fresh air felt.

"Do you know how it feels—to just breathe again? You forget how . . . oh, sweet Lord," she said, and just kept taking deep breaths. "Now I'm going to tell you a secret. It's about those boxes you're getting, and those pictures. And those coffins. What they mean . . ."

Just then, the phone rang in the other part of the house.

This time, there was no gradual shimmer about it: Bonnie was immediately gone.

Vanished.

And Alice was there in seconds, to take her place. Standing at the door, holding the gun, and saying, "Some crazy woman's on the phone, saying she's calling for *that man.*"

That man could only be one person.

Alice pointed with the gun at the cup of coffee that was on Nelle's nightstand, next to the Bible. Steam rose off it.

"With libations like that, you won't ever go to sleep."

But had she been asleep at all?

Chapter Sixteen

At first, Nelle thought the woman must be calling to say Truman
was dead—why else would she call in the middle of the night?—
but no, she was just apologizing for sending snake guts.

"He made me send that box. I'd never put snake parts through
the U.S. Postal Service. It's not Christian. It's not right." Saying "it's
not right" made Myrtle start crying again; it's not right she was
going to die, that's why she was calling. She had to line up somebody to take care of Truman. She didn't want to die with him, or
snake guts, on her conscience.

Nelle could have used another cup of coffee; where was Bonnie Clutter when she needed her, to make a fresh pot? Nelle was still in a daze. She barely knew what was being said, or what she was saying in return, before she heard herself saying it.

"Is he there now? Truman? Put him on, I've about had it with these boxes . . ."

"He's out like a light . . . he'd have a fit if he knew I called. Had to sneak away. Must have given you some sort of shock, opening that box . . ."

There she goes again, with those damn snake guts.

"Then why'd you send it!" Really. This woman. People had to take some responsibility for what they did. "How'd *you* feel if you opened up something like that? I haven't heard from him in twenty years and now he sends me something like that. Those . . . boxes. Coffins. Pictures. If he wants something, just tell me . . ."

"You know Truman . . ."

No, she didn't, not anymore.

". . . has to say ten words when one'll do just fine, thank you very much. Ten you can't even figure out anyway, they got so many curlicues on 'em. Anybody else, they'd just send those boxes back . . ."

"How could I? I didn't even know they were from him, not for sure . . . I don't have an address . . ."

". . . forget the boxes . . . you're the only one even takes his calls anymore."

That stopped Nelle.

"Even in the middle of the night, you never hung up on him. All those other people did, those people used to brag he was their friend and such . . ."

And Nelle had been about to hang up on this woman, calling in the middle of the night.

Sometimes, that's the only time you could send out a call for help.

Just like Bonnie Clutter, this woman was searching for what she wanted to say, ten words when one would have done: help.

"He's acting crazy these days, saying ghosts comin' to get him . . ."

Days ago, Nelle would have laughed.

Now, this very night—why is this night different from all other nights?—she'd just had coffee with Bonnie Clutter.

That's why it was different.

"Only ghost around here is Truman, he's so full of liquor and pills. Fadin' before my very eyes. I don't know what to do anymore. He's outta his head . . . why else would he put a dead snake in a box . . ."

"He hates snakes. One bit him when he was little, he almost died . . ."

"Got 'em all over the house now, stuffed ones, carved ones, fake ones, but he had Mr. Danny haul that one up, after we went out in the desert looking for a sign from Nancy."

She said it like it was the most natural thing in the world.

Days ago, Nelle would have laughed at that, too.

Now, she wanted to cry, after all her nightly visitors.

"But what does he *want?* Those pictures he puts in . . . even got somebody to put one of them in a grave. A grave. Where somebody had died. If that's not plum illegal . . ."

Myrtle hadn't known that.

Where somebody had died.

Death.

Her own.

It's why she had called, she couldn't forget that. She had business to accomplish, but now it seemed hopeless: would *you* take somebody in who'd been sending you coffins through the mail?

"He's ramblin' all the time now, and I don't know if he's talking to me, or somebody I can't see. This house is getting too crowded, and as far as I can see, there's just the two of us in it, and pretty soon it's just gonna be the one . . ."

"You've gotta wake him up . . . I'm gonna put an end to this . . ."

". . . and now he's going on about this party and I know he's gonna wear himself out even more . . ."

"What party?"

". . . and nobody'll come anyway. He wants to throw this big bash, just like that black-and-white thing. See, he just got his book back . . ."

"What book?"

"He says it's the part everybody's waitin' for . . . he says it's the last thing he's ever gonna write, 'sides a suicide note. Got it with him right now, that book, hugging it and snorin', won't let it out of his sight . . . says you're the only one he trusts with it, you'll know what to do, the graveyard, all the answers are there, back where it all started, he's not making any sense far as I can tell . . ."

Then another voice, in another room:

"Myrtle, get me my pills . . . the blue ones . . . and the orange ones . . . and get this damn dog off me, I'm covered with dog slobber . . . Goddamn it, Maggie . . ."

"Oh, Lord, he's wakin' up now . . ."

Oh, Lord, Myrtle thought, now I'm never gonna get anybody to take care of him.

"Please. Let me just talk to him . . ."

Now it was Nelle's turn to cry for help, in the middle of the night.

"I'll call later . . ."

"No, wait, please, just give me your number . . ."

But the phone went dead.

Nelle was left to her anger and sadness and confusion: she didn't know anything more about the boxes, but she knew Truman had a new book, and a party in the wings, and some kind of answer, back at the graveyard. Or was this a dream, too? Would she wake up in the morning and see the phone cord in her hand, and have no idea how it got there? How could two people, once best friends, once soul mates, be so different: Nelle had published one book, and then deliberately faded into the woodwork; Truman didn't even wait for one to come out, and had already started planning the guest list.

She'd barely made the first guest list.

She was about to lose her mind: *what did he want?*

Ed would know what to do, he'd know what it all meant.

She went back to her bedroom and took the writing tablet from under the Bible on her bedside table; tonight, she didn't feel like climbing up to the attic.

Tonight, for the first time in quite a while, she was afraid of the dark.

> *My Dearest Ed:*
> *Are you mad at me, Big Brother? Please say no. Big Sister Bear is; in the morning, she'll come grumbling into the room, her fur all cinched up in righteous indignation, to let me know she didn't appreciate my late night phone call.*
> *Do you mind my late night call to you?*
> *It is strange, being visited by these ghosts of people I came to know so well on paper, but never knew in real life. And never being visited by the ghosts of those I knew best in flesh and blood, like you or Mother or Amasa. Or do you come to me, in ways I don't realize—the ongoing conversation we have in my head when I write you a letter, or the strange dreams that came for years after you died? You*

know I'd be a receptive audience, as I hope I was with Bonnie Clutter. Did I do right by her? You must tell me how to act around ghosts, I don't know. I don't want to do the wrong thing. (Am I better at socializing with the dead than I am the living? Maybe that's why everybody's so scared of me, and I'm so scared of them.)

There are many things on my mind tonight, many fears, but while it is uppermost, I want to write on the subject of parties.

A strange topic, you might think, for this twilight time between waking and sleeping.

Not really; I think of parties, and what comes to my mind is the time I was in between, neither started nor finished.

I think of the night Truman almost finished the act of killing me, that he had started in Kansas.

I feel as if I've been left hanging in between ever since.

Everybody thinks my "missing years" are the ones long after The Book came out, but they're really just the few years after I fled Kansas in the middle of the night, until Truman's Black and White Ball.

I saw Truman several times, during those in-between years, but we never mentioned what had happened that night, not in words, at least. But in every look that passed between us, it was the only subject.

I don't know why I even talked to him again, but I did.

Maybe I was as lonely as he was.

Back in New York, we went to Sardi's and had cold potato soup and took the Deweys to see "Hello Dolly" and "The Odd Couple": the odd couple, it's what people must have called me and Truman, behind our backs.

I was doing just fine getting my name in the paper, same as him, whether I wanted it there or not. (He certainly did, no disputing that.) I went to the teas and the chicken ala king luncheons in my honor; I talked to the reporters who thought I was a man until I showed up in person, and probably still thought so after I left. I sent money when somebody needed to defend my book against being "immoral"; I read about the church in Chattanooga that buried it as a "strange god"—along with short shorts, TV sets, and clocks—a harbinger of a modern age they didn't want. (Little did they know, I didn't want it either. At least I was in good company; they buried Steinbeck alongside me. That's the closest I ever got to meeting old Johnny.) I got myself invited to the opening of the Kennedy Center; I even had my picture taken with Lady Bird, who told me she liked a good book as much as a big piece of steak.

I did all those things; I was famous, for a while.

I was famous until Truman thought I was too famous.

Months before the Black and White Ball—bear with me, Brother, I'm getting to where Truman almost kills me, again—he started harping on what I should wear. Harping on Harper, he called it. I'd planned on wearing my good black suit; it had been good enough to get me my job at the airlines, good enough to bury our father in, and it would be good enough for Truman. I couldn't imagine myself in a gown; I'd look like a circus freak, trying to get all buttercupped up and looking even more freakish. A giant, trying to look demure. I'd wear the strand of pearls Mother left me, and there you have it—Black and White, just like the invitation requested.

"No," screamed Truman, as if it were the last sound he would ever make, and he had to make it count. "A suit? A black suit? I am not going to have you meet all my important New York friends done up in something you wore to a funeral. It'll smell like death—you can't get that stench off no matter how hard you try, I know, sister, I've tried—and I want you to smell like life. Because that's what I'm starting, a new life. With this book, I can tell."

He dragged me, kicking and screaming, to the same places his fancy lady friends went—to the salon of Mr. Kenneth, who took one terrified look at the mop on top of my head and said not even he could do anything with it; to

Tiffany's, where Truman had thought about holding the ball; to Bendel's, for a fairytale gown . . .

It was all too rich for my blood, and I told him so: "I'll look like somebody took pity on an old abandoned dog and stuck a tacky circus costume on it to cheer it up. I'll look ridiculous wearing all that fancy stuff. Don't worry, I'll find something decent to wear . . ."

He screamed at me once more, even louder than before.

"Decent won't do! This is the party to end all parties! If you can't make a little effort to pull yourself together for it, then we'll just see if you make the final cut or not. Just maybe you will, maybe you won't . . ."

And to think this had all begun when four people, four decent, innocent people, had their brains blown out.

He pulled out the little notebook that all of New York high society lived in mortal fear of in those days, jotted down a notation, and wagged it at me.

What had he written: "Nelle won't play dress-up the way I want her to, so I'm not gonna invite her"?

I was tired of playing dress-up for Truman.

I'd been doing it since I was six years old, when I'd climbed a chinaberry tree with him to watch Halloween come and go, taking our childhoods with it. But I wasn't six years old anymore. I was famous now, too. My book had made a splash, so had its movie. I'd won the Pulitzer; Truman hadn't, yet, although he was certain it was coming his way. I deserved my own party, and in one of the rare moments of indulgence I allowed myself, I fantasized that Truman was giving the party—for me.

It would be my little secret.

It would get me through the night.

I'd wear the mask he requested, but behind it, I'd be the true belle of the ball. (Imagine me, the belle of anybody's ball.)

And it came to pass: once people found out who I was— the dreamy-eyed girl hiding in the grass on a book jacket, now grown up and wearing a ridiculous long black dress— they couldn't get enough of me.

Once they found out Truman was my Dill Harris, that strange little creature who came to visit us every summer, they really couldn't get enough of me.

And once they found out I'd helped Truman on In Cold Blood, *going there in the snow and talking to all those folks, they almost lost their minds. (I longed for them to take off their masks so I'd know who I was talking to, but Truman was on the prowl: if he saw anyone remove their masks before the appointed time at midnight, he ran out of the receiving line and snapped it back into place. When they winced at the sting of rubber band against flesh, he said, "Let that be a reminder to you to do as you've been told.")*

I introduced them all to Al Dewey—I called him Foxy to tease him, just as we had back in Kansas—and said, "this is the man who solved the crime and put Dick and Perry behind bars." Then I paused and said, "And this is his wife, who kept them there." That always got a laugh, even though I didn't really know what it meant.

The Deweys looked as elegant as anyone there.

Soon, everyone forgot about wanting to visit with Truman at all, forsaking him for me, and my campfire tales of the Clutters and murder on the Plains.

Did you see the house?

Did you see the blood?

Did the police really burn the mattress Nancy got killed on?

Did you meet the killers?

What were they like?

Pure evil?

Did you know Truman would grow up to be famous?

("Wait," I interrupted, "are we still talking about pure evil, or Truman?" That got a laugh, too.)

Soon, I had a receiving line as long as Truman's and Mrs. Graham's, the Washington Post owner and guest of honor. I excused myself to the ladies' room to catch a breath, and try to cool down the fever of the crowd and their questions. I shoved my mask on top of my head; it was a black sleep mask I'd swiped from Truman and cut eye holes in, even though women were supposed to wear white, another fashion faux pas I'd never live down. I splashed my face with cold water—you know me, no makeup to worry about—and felt the same sting of cold against hot I'd felt that night in Kansas.

I should have known that was an omen.

I looked in the mirror and talked to myself.

"This is my party. This is my party. I have a Pulitzer prize and he doesn't."

It was the first time in my life I'd ever said it aloud.

It was like somebody else was talking.

Only then did I notice an attendant in the bathroom. As soon as I saw her, in the mirror, she looked down, as if to say "I didn't hear a word you said."

"I. am. mortified. I didn't mean . . . I know it's his party . . . I was just joking."

She didn't know what I was talking about, and even if she had, she wouldn't have cared.

She offered a tray, covered with objects in black or white: washcloths, combs, hand soaps, even breath mints—everything stamped with the ornate "P" of the Plaza Hotel. I picked up one of the soaps, and saw that the back was stamped with "TC."

Truman had infiltrated even the bathrooms.

The black soaps smelled like licorice.

I took a white soap and sniffed it: vanilla, a scent that was always in the air of the kitchen Truman grew up in. (You might remember our mother never cooked; we were always having to go next door to get a decent meal.)

"They're souvenirs. You s'posed to keep 'em," the ladies' maid said. "I already got a pocketful. Gonna try to sell 'em to those autograph hounds out in the rain."

Trying to escape my embarrassment, I put the white soap in my bag and went out, trying to brush the wax from *it off on the back of my dress, even though the maid was already snapping out a hand towel—black or white, of course, the choice was mine.*

When I got back to the ballroom, the stroke of midnight had come and gone: masks had been removed, guests had begun eating. Chicken hash with sherry, omelettes, and caviar—birds and eggs, Truman went around chirping, when he wasn't chirping that his mask had cost just thirty-nine cents at Kresge's. (And that's when he wasn't chirping how he got paid $14.80 a word for In Cold Blood, since he'd made over two million on it.)

I thought back to Truman's good-bye Halloween party when he was seven, how it was really no different from this: word of it had gone out around town, and it had grown to become the thing everybody wanted to attend. And Truman had asserted his power by keeping everyone guessing to the last possible minute who got in, and who didn't. Standing there at the front door, he was host and gatekeeper, judge and jury, all at once. Truman, guarding the gate. It's what he's always done.

Finally, unmasked, I could see who'd been pelting me with questions all night long: Frank Sinatra and Mia Farrow, Candice Bergen, Lauren Bacall, Jerome Robbins, princes and princesses and kings and queens of countries I'd never heard of. Secret Service men, guarding Lady Bird and her daughters. Tall cotton indeed.

It may have started out as a fantasy, but now, it was a reality: I was the belle of the ball.

"May I?"

I was yanked out of my fantasy when a rubber band hit my skull.

I guess pride does goeth before a fall.

It was Truman, reaching toward the sleep mask I'd forgotten and left on top of my head, making my hair bunch up into something even more unattractive than it had started out as.

"Don't wanna look foolish, do we?"

In his sleight of hand, he managed to give it an extra-hard snap as he pulled it off and stuck it in his pocket.

"I'll just take what's rightfully mine."

He leaned closer, whispering into my right ear, which was weighted down by a ridiculous earring on loan from his Mr. Kenneth.

Truman's accent was stronger than it had ever been in his life.

"Sistah, you're stealin' my thunder."

That's all he said before he grabbed Lauren Bacall by the waist—a forkful of omelette halfway to her mouth, a question to me still hanging in the air—and yanked her onto the dance floor.

No one else had seen it.

I didn't think anyone else had heard it, what Truman told my new friend Miss Betty Bacall, as she'd told me to call her:

"Poor little thing," I imagined Truman saying, "I practic'ly had to write her book for her. Why else d'you think I'm in it?"

Betty Bacall looked at me, a feeble, uncertain smile.

Truman looked very certainly at me, sticking out his tongue like a snake, then darting it back into his mouth to poke at his cheeks.

That's all it took for the rumor to begin and take hold, just like the roots of the chinaberry tree in which we'd first huddled so many years ago, after Truman's first triumphant party.

I couldn't take those feeble, uncertain smiles that followed, the questions in their eyes.

I left, but not before I'd dropped the small white soap in Truman's drink, for him to wash his mouth out with.

Little good it did; the rumor took hold, and has lasted till this very day.

It's all poor Alice ever thinks about.

I can only ever write this to you, very late at night.

I've never told anyone before.

He made me think I didn't write It, when I knew I had.
He killed me, as sure as Dick and Perry killed the Clutters.

Nelle put the pen down, the callused sides of her writing fingers smeared with ink. Her hand was worn out, but no more than her brain and her pride, and she couldn't write anything more to Ed.

That was the last time she'd seen Truman.

When she got back to Monroeville, she was asked to write an article on the party for the local paper, the very paper her father had once owned. One of the town's very own, at the party of the decade. Even then, Truman had begun lopping branches off the family tree; no one from his family in Monroeville had been invited. She declined, saying, with a mischievous smile, that what happened at the party stayed at the party, like she'd just come off furlough on a ship with the Merchant Marine.

But despite the painful memories, Nelle did keep her invitation, and the shell of a silver balloon she'd taken on her way out (and popped, with a glittering bobby pin she'd seen fall out of Marianne Moore's hair).

She'd kept one other souvenir from that evening: a silver napkin that had been dabbed with lipstick—not her own, God forbid, but Betty Bacall's, just before Truman had waltzed her away and whispered into her ear.

—

It was hours before the sun came up, but Nelle was all ready to go out: to the graveyard, where Myrtle had seemed to indicate Truman had left the answers.

Answers to what, she didn't know, although she could guess:

Why he'd gone even more crazy at this juncture in his life.

Why she seemed to be following him there, giving any of her time to a man who had so rejected her.

For once, she thought Alice might be right: it was the telephone's fault. Alice had said it would be the end of them; she'd said that the very day they'd had it installed. And her prediction had come to pass: those calls from Truman, this last call from Myrtle . . . it was the end of something.

So was what Nelle was doing now: sneaking into her sister's bedroom to take the gun that sleeping Alice had left by the side of her bed.

There was too much sneaking around in the house, but Nelle made a silent promise this would be the end of it: whatever she found at the cemetery, whether it was something, or nothing . . . that would be the end.

To keep her company, to keep her safe, she took the letter she'd just finished to Ed, the snake boxes and photos, and the gun.

Truman had taught her very well indeed: if you introduced a gun into a story, somewhere, somehow, it had to go off.

Chapter Seventeen

"He's a fag, you know. Yag. Gay."

Truman hated saying the word, so he always inverted it.

"Yag as a goose."

He'd woken up in the middle of Myrtle's SOS call to Nelle, but now that it was really bedtime, he couldn't go back to sleep. The blue late-night-TV light flickered over him as he sat on the couch, jotting down ideas for his party and watching Johnny Carson.

"Who's 'yag'?"

"Johnny Carson. He and Doc Severinsen, they're lovers."

He said it without a shade of inflection, no gossipy delight, just a statement of fact. He couldn't even take delight in his lying anymore, he was so drugged out. And if there's one thing Myrtle knew, it was that Johnny Carson wasn't a fag. Doc Severinsen, now, she wasn't altogether sure about him.

"And those clothes, just hideous. All those stripes and polyester."

Myrtle was trying to figure out how to tell Truman she was dying, and all he wanted to talk about was Johnny Carson being a fag, a poorly dressed fag at that.

Truman was one to talk, lying there in shorts and an old T-shirt, his belly hanging out, coffee stains all over him. Myrtle had begged him to let her wash the shorts, but he'd refused, saying they were his good luck shorts: since he'd been wearing them when his book had been returned, he was certain that if he kept wearing them, he'd be able to do some new writing. He just had a few more chapters to go, he had it all mapped out, he'd practically memorized it.

It's what he'd been telling people for years.

Because without a new book, there couldn't be a new party.

For a brief time, he'd had a change of plans about it. Instead of an Arabian Nights setting, he wanted it to take place in Paraguay circa 1830, with everyone dressed like Spanish royalty. And not just set there, but actually *take place* there; everyone would have to fly to Paraguay, a place Truman had never been, for the party. But Myrtle had her heart set on the Arabian Nights, after Truman's stories of harems and belly dancers and incense; she took one look at his Paraguayan pictures and told him she didn't think he'd look all that good cinched up in a cummerbund like that.

"You're right. What horrible clothes . . ."

"See, I told ya . . . you don't wanna be all hemmed in like that . . ."

"No, Johnny. All that polyester. Just horrible."

He was back on the King of Late Night, putting his party pad down.

"I can smell it through the TV screen. Can't you smell that? Just look at it: checks on the pants, stripes on the shirt, more stripes on the tie, plaids going every which way . . . no wonder Joanne divorced him. How could you live with a man who dresses like that?"

Now that Truman had run everybody else out of his life, except Myrtle, Joanne Carson was the only one left who ever called or came to visit. She was Johnny's ex-wife, and Truman had adopted her when they both lived at the UN Plaza in New York. He'd played Henry Higgins to her Eliza Doolittle, and tried to make her a part of café society.

"You know, he beat her," Truman said, again matter-of-factly, as he sat there hypnotized by Charo trying to explain how to make coq au vin to Richard Chamberlain, shaking her tits as if they were part of the recipe. "Never let her go out. If it hadn't been for me, she'd still be there. In that apartment. Captive. While he was out buying polyester."

Polyester.

And she was dying.

"He needs me as a guest . . . this is one of the worst shows in the history of TV. You know why I'm such a good guest, Myrtle?"

"No, why are you such a good guest?" she asked, when what she wanted to scream was, "Don't you ever notice anything but yourself?"

"Because I tell the truth. I'm the only person in the world who goes on these shows and tells the truth. People can tell it, they can sniff the truth a mile away. You can smell it worse than polyester. Every single one of 'em, liars . . . Richard Chamberlain, lying through his pearly whites. Charo, lying through those double-D tits a Beverly Hills surgeon stuck on her. She's even lying about her Goddamn recipe. You and me, Myrtle, we're the only ones who tell the truth, no matter who it hurts."

He hadn't told the truth since God knows when.

And he wouldn't let her tell the truth to him, no matter how hard she tried.

"Call Johnny right now, get him on the phone, it's in my address book, I'm gonna book myself right now, they need a dose of the truth. Get on a plane right now . . ."

But a few minutes later, Truman had already forgotten he wanted to be on the show, because Charo had started singing "The Windmills of Your Mind."

It was one of his favorite songs that year.

When The Amazing Kreskin came on as the third guest of the evening, Truman claimed he was gay, too; he'd even slept with him. "He wasn't any good 'cause he kept reading my mind. There wasn't any mystery. No suspense. You can't have good sex without suspense."

He was lonely for Mr. Danny.

That was the only truth going on in that room, but Truman would never say it.

As long as Truman and Myrtle kept the TV on, the ghosts, alive as well as dead, would stay away.

—

Thank God Nelle had worn her tennis shoes; by the time she walked all the way to the cemetery on the outskirts of town, she was exhausted. She'd be surprised if her feet weren't bleeding, even though she'd sliced open the sides of her tennis shoes with razor blades to make way for her bunions.

Cinderella, running away from the Black and White Ball, with bunions.

She didn't care anymore. She'd been a good girl, and now she was tired, and angry.

She carried the gun from Kansas with her to deal with her anger.

The front gate to the cemetery was locked, so she tossed her bag of goodies over the short brick fence and scrambled over it like she used to when she was little and wasn't afraid of things. It hurt, but it was a good hurt; because it took her straight back to childhood: through the soft rubber of the worn soles, she could feel the diamonds of metal that crosshatched the fence, feel her toes curling for a better grip, her fists searching for just the right handhold between the sharp spikes that ran along the top of the fence. The spikes were there to keep the wrong people out; with a gun and a bag full of oddities, as if to perform voodoo, she was definitely one of the wrong people.

A patch of moonlight had followed her all the way, her only friend right now, in the still of the night. How many times had that patch of quiet moonlight helped her pass the night, when words wouldn't come. It didn't talk back to her, like Alice, didn't tell her everything was going to be all right, didn't tell her that she was going to finish her book one day. It didn't say or do anything, but somehow, it comforted her; it just stayed there—in the sky, on the wall, through the trees—night after night, never fail.

That's all she wanted from a friend: consistency.

It was more than she'd gotten from Truman.

In the cemetery, she expected ghosts; instead, she got moon-light. But it was like a ghost in a way, an old friend that had come back after a gap of decades. It had been there in her New York walk-up the whole time she was writing The Book, a harbinger of that delicious time of night when everything went quiet, even the New York traffic, and she could finally hear the voices in her head. When Boo and Scout and Jem and Atticus and Calpurnia and Miss Maudie bubbled up, eager to tell their stories. She prayed for that time, when the only light was a square of moonlight on the wall, coming in through her tiny window.

Bit by bit, she'd move her attention from that square of moon-light to the square of paper in front of her; she'd begin filling it with words, and only know it was time to stop when, hours later, she had a saucer full of cigarette butts. That was her alarm clock; only then was it time to go to work. She'd drag in exhausted because she'd been up all night writing; sometimes she'd go in just as exhausted when she hadn't written a word, but had been up all night knowing she should.

And during the day, all she could think about was coming back home at night to that square of moonlight.

Now, that same patch of moonlight, as old and weary as her, showed her the way, deep into the cemetery to her brother Ed's tombstone. She had a new letter to show him, along with the other strange gods that had come to haunt her.

—

In a commercial break between The Amazing Kreskin and Erik Estrada, Myrtle got Truman to let her put his "lucky shorts" in the wash. She didn't know how lucky they were, just dirty, with slobber and stiff bristly hairs and paw prints from Maggie all over them. Finally, she couldn't stand it anymore: she told Truman if he wanted a girl when he woke up in the morning—meaning her—then he better strip down now, because she couldn't stand the filth anymore. She didn't care if his show wasn't over; the shorts were beginning to smell, and she was about to gag.

Truman changed to long pants, fiddling with buttons and zippers while his eyes never left the TV and the gold cross around Erik Estrada's neck. "He could play Perry in a remake," Truman mumbled to himself.

When Myrtle came back from running a wash, the smell of chlorine replacing the smell of dog, Erik Estrada had been replaced by Bernadette Peters, who was singing "Thank You for Being a Friend" and shaking her moppet red curls at the camera. Johnny looked "bemused" watching her; that had become one of Truman's favorite words lately, and Myrtle had started using it as well.

"That girl sure does 'bemuse' me; I'd give anything to have Kewpie doll lips like her," Myrtle said, then turned to get a reaction from Truman at her improving vocabulary.

Only Truman wasn't there.

A dry wind outside blew the front door open and shut, as Bernadette took a bow to applause.

A few pages from Truman's book scattered up in the breeze. Myrtle grabbed them, and then had a moment of conscience over whether she should look at what Truman had guarded so carefully. As she hesitated, more pages circled around her, and she just started grabbing and looking without thinking. She finally saw what his closely guarded magnum opus consisted of.

It was worse than she had feared; not the quality of the writing, but what was on the pages themselves.

The pages whipped up outside, the only specks of light pulling her into a pitch black night, pulling her toward Truman.

—

Someone once said to Nelle, after Ed had passed, "Where's your brother?" She looked at them a full minute in disbelief—they knew Ed had died—until they repeated the question differently: "Where's he *buried?*"

Oh.

That.

Ed was here, in the graveyard.

Truman's people weren't.

The Faulks, his mother's people, were buried elsewhere, and his father's people were in New Orleans.

Nelle had been living in New York just a short while when Truman's mother died. Truman himself was in Paris when it happened; he later joked how appropriate that was, since his mother's favorite perfume had been Evening in Paris. He thought she'd arranged it like that, so he'd never forget.

He hated her and she hated him; he said he doubted he could have forgotten that, no matter where he was at the time.

The polite story was that she died of pneumonia, but everyone knew. Everyone knew she lived beyond her means; everyone knew she'd changed her name from Lillie Mae to Nina when she moved from New Orleans to Park Avenue; everyone knew her new husband, Joe Capote, embezzled money from his job to keep her happy. And everyone knew Joe was going to Sing Sing, now that his employers had found out. There was no way around that, famous stepson to bail him out or not. Nina couldn't handle it; she took a bottle of pills to bail herself out.

Someone called Truman in Paris to let him know; he took a seventeen-hour transatlantic night flight back, crying most of the way, even if he hated her.

Evening in Paris, indeed.

He wouldn't cry again until Dick and Perry were executed.

Truman wanted Nelle to ride in the limousine as part of the family, on the way to the funeral at Frank Campbell's. Joe Capote threw a fit, said she's my wife, I'm paying, I'm deciding.

Truman said, "Can an embezzler say 'I'm paying' with a straight face?"

Nelle rode in the limo with the family.

Very few of Truman's family made the trip up north, scandalized because Truman was going to have his mother cremated. "Every so often, you have to give your memory a little lobotomy, and that's what I'm going to do, cut them out one by one . . . cut out the past."

Nelle was a part of that past; it was the first time she'd wondered if he'd eventually do the same to her.

They huddled in a bar after the service, knocking back Kentucky bourbon.

"I hate her, I hate what she did to me. I gave her all this, why did she do . . . she's never accepted me. You know that time I wrote you? In high school? I came home and somebody had written 'Capote the Fag' on the door? She said it was a delivery boy. I bet it was her. She hated me. Her own son. Well, damn her."

He paused, gulping fire from the South.

"Nelle, I'm going to be famous."

She didn't know if that continued from the previous thought—
"Well, damn her"—or just existed on its own, a non sequitur never
far from Truman's mind.

"It's all I've ever wanted, and I got it from her. It's the one
fucking thing she gave me."

He chewed on an ice cube to put out the fire.

"I should have been a girl."

Gulping her own fire, Nelle joked, "And I should've been a boy."

A memory before it happened, a memory of the fire to come,
in a bar in Kansas.

"We should just switch and be each other. That would solve
all the problems. C'mon, we're going. Put the bourbon in your
purse."

He took them to the Latin Quarter in the West Fifties, using his
velvet funeral suit and Kentucky mash to push his way through the
crowds outside, already well-known enough to get in without
waiting.

"We're gonna dance our way so far away from all this."

The day he buried his mother, and he was swing dancing
with the most leaden partner there, telling the orchestra leader
to pick up the tempo. When a slow dance came up, Nelle
assumed he'd want to sit that one out, but he held onto her even
harder.

His whispering mouth barely reached her ear.

"Never leave me, Nelle, you're the only one who understands.
Promise."

He didn't wait for an answer; years later, he would be the one
to leave her.

They only sat down ringside when the entertainment came
on: Christine Jorgensen, the "convertible blonde" who had started

out life as a man. She launched into "I Enjoy Being a Girl," kicking up her svelte and shapely legs; Truman squealed and clapped.

By the time she got to her finale, it was as if she were singing only to him. Tears streamed down his face, and he mouthed the noble words along with her: "When you walk through the storm, hold your head up high . . ."

This woman who used to be a man, getting Truman to cry.

"Nelly, I should'a been a girl."

"And I should'a been a boy."

They were both crying now.

Thoughts of shape-shifting late at night, in a cemetery.

There were no Capotes in this graveyard, only Nelle couldn't escape them, wherever she went.

She hurried on to Ed's grave.

—

Myrtle threw on a sweater and went outside; should she get something else to cover Truman? He'd just been wearing pants and a T-shirt, unless he'd put on something else. The car was still there, so he must have gone somewhere on foot. It was cold out in the desert around their house; as hot as it was during the day, it was cold at night.

She grabbed a scrap quilt that Truman's cousin Sook had made long ago; normally, it was the padding on a bench right by the door. She'd drape it around Truman's shoulders when she found him. He used to point to the intricate designs on it and tell Myrtle every one of them had a meaning; they were secrets only he and Sook could interpret. Some cold day, he kept promising, he and Myrtle would wrap up in it, and he'd explain what it all meant.

He'd better hurry up with it, unless he planned on it being her shroud. Then, she'd have all the time in the world to figure it out for herself.

Damn it!

Not now.

She had things to do.

First, find Truman. Then she'd worry about dying.

She didn't have a good feeling about this.

Truman was afraid of the dark; he wouldn't have gone out there by himself if he was in his right mind, which he seldom was these days. Between his ghosts and his pills, she didn't know which was worse. No, she didn't have a good feeling about this at all.

And the pages she'd seen from his book hadn't helped.

Maggie pawed at the screen door behind her, thinking it was time for her walk. But Myrtle wouldn't get anywhere if she had to be on the watch for Truman and the dog both, worried a hyena or hawk would swoop down and take off with it, so she left Maggie behind. Let the dog watch TV; it was still on, a blue beacon through the window. Maybe it was like an evening star that would guide Truman back home from wherever he had gone.

Suddenly, a light hit her in the face; thank God, there he is! At least he'd had the good sense to take a flashlight. But then the light shifted, and in its aura, she could see the face behind it— not Truman, but Mr. Danny.

She was glad to see even him, but she couldn't let him know that.

"What you do with Truman?"

"Whaddaya mean? I just got here."

"He's missing. Wouldn't be the first thing you took didn't belong to you."

"I brought the book back. I came to say I was sorry."

That reminded Myrtle of what she'd done to his car; she was sorry, too. With the weight of her own mortality on her shoulders, she thought she better set things right first, then look for Truman second.

"I'm sorry 'bout your car. You get it runnin' okay?"

"You see me standin' here? I didn't walk all the way."

"You're damn lucky he didn't come after the caps on your teeth. I had to talk him out of that one."

"I still care for Truman, you know."

"You got a funny way of showing it."

"He's a hell of a lot more fun than my wife is."

"Don't know if I like hearing that."

"Sometimes you gotta hear things you don't want to."

He paused, then asked the question that was still on his mind.

"You read any of that book of his?"

Myrtle paused.

"Some pages of it blew away when he took off. Yeah, I looked at 'em."

And she wished she hadn't.

The book he was planning the biggest party in the world over, at least from the evidence of the few pages at hand, wouldn't make for anything.

It was the single word *heliotrope* typed over and over, turned into its own crossword.

Danny spoke up.

"You know that word?"

"Yeah."

"You know what it means?"

"No."

"I looked it up."

That's a scene Myrtle would have liked to have seen.

"'Heliotrope.' It's a sunflower that faces the sun."

"Nothing wrong with that, just . . . Truman knows a lot more words. Why'd he keep using that one over and over?"

"It's something else, too. A color."

"What kinda color?"

He aimed his flashlight at the night sky around them: "Sorta like this."

Heliotrope: the sky was reddish purple, the color of blood.

—

It looked different at night, Ed's grave. The flecks of shiny marble and granite on the surface of the tombstone picked up the moon-light and sparkled in a way they didn't during the day.

In the light of the moon, it seemed to glow.

Nelle put down her bag on the plot of land and began pulling out items from it. Oh, how she would have laughed, or shivered, if she'd been able to float above and look down on the scene: an old woman with gray hair, in the middle of the night, laying out the artifacts of her necromancy on a grave. She'd become the witch everyone already said she was. She hadn't known what she was going to do with them when she left the house; she still didn't know, exactly. Probably bury the things and get them out of her life forever. She'd gone up to her attic office and with one unceremo-nious, backhanded swipe of her fist, knocked them all into a K-mart shopping bag.

Once—in her childhood? In her mind? In a book, a movie?—she had kept a worn cigar box filled with precious mementoes like this: a pocket watch, cat's-eye marbles, Indian-head pennies, rubbed-down crayons, the figures of a boy and a girl carved from soap.

They had come from a stranger, who watched her from afar.

Now, the play pretties she carried were considerably more grown up, and much scarier, although they had come from a watcher in the woods as well: Truman, who had been there at the very beginning, when she wanted to find surprises in a tree. She thought back to one of the most useful lessons he had ever taught her about writing, a single question: what story are you telling? He said that's the only question a writer had to ask himself; once you knew that answer, the book wrote itself. He'd also said, write what you know. To which she said, but we don't know the Clutters, so why are we writing about them? He answered in kind, because I want to know them. They seem like good people. It was one of the kindest, truest things she'd ever heard come out of his mouth.

Now, she wanted to ask him the same question: what story are you telling?

She laid out the items Truman had sent, fanning them out in three rows, like instruments for a surgical procedure, or tarot cards, waiting for a sorceress to reveal their hidden meanings.

First, the photographs:

Her tending this very grave, unaware of having her picture taken.

Truman and her in the Clutters' basement, just weeks after the murders.

Her entering the courthouse in Jefferson City, working on a book about a killer that would never be finished.

That night in Kansas City, in the snow, with the Nyes; a "night on the town she'd never forget," Truman had said, before he killed a part of her forever.

Just pictures, snapshots from her life: grief and a kind of death the common denominator in all of them, no matter what they seemed to show on the surface.

Next, the three small hand-carved coffins, one of which had come filled with earth, one inlaid with red velvet that might have come from a dead girl's prom dress, one with a snake's rattle.

Finally, in the row closest to her, the strangest of all: the snakebite kits, with their bizarre collages. She lined them up, one after another, in the order she had received them . . . and there it was, plain as day, the story he was telling.

It was an image of the Clutters' grave, and she'd missed it the whole time, even though it had been right in front of her. Not quite a picture, or a photograph, it was more like a dream landscape, a portrait constructed through the filter of memory. Once the three boxes were lined up together, their sides touching, the tops and largest front panels formed one unbroken panorama that had been cut into three equal puzzle pieces, all adding up to the fight they had had at Nancy's grave, when he told her he was going to make up the ending of the book and turn a scene of violence into a scene of peace and moving on.

There was one large grave marker with four separate scribbles on it.

There was a giant tree, its roots spreading deep down, under the coffins.

There was a chestnut horse, Babe, Nancy's horse, rearing on its hind legs in the distance.

There was the hint of green grass, and the spring to come, but covered with a dusting of pearly gray snow.

There were two people, a man and a woman, one short, the

other tall, a boy and a girl lost in the past who shivered as they looked down at it all.

And there was a snake that seemed to be burrowing down ever farther, lower than the roots of the tree.

On the tombstone, there was scribbling that looked like the Rosetta stone, telling her that these were all clues to be deciphered.

But what did they mean?

The same question she'd been asking since day one; she knew the story, but what did it add up to?

It couldn't mean that Truman had actually buried something there, at the Clutters' grave, could it? Not even he would go that far, to desecrate the final resting place of the young girl whose death had shaken him so.

Would he?

He played fast and loose with a lot, but not with Nancy's memory. It had almost killed him to write about her murder; he'd wept as he called Nelle from Switzerland after finishing it, just needing to talk to someone. He told her if science ever came up with a kind of fingerprint powder for words—and could lift the very last things the Clutters had breathed to themselves off the insides of the tape that had gone over their mouths—he wouldn't want to know what it was. He couldn't bear to see those bubbles of spit and prayer and terror.

But was Truman telling Nelle to go there now and find out if something more was buried there, other than the memory of a huge fight they'd had, under the spreading arms of a beautiful oak tree . . .

She was working too hard on this, thinking it added up to something, when, if Myrtle was right, Truman was just crazy these days, and it added up to nothing. But something festered in her.

This was too precise for that. As much of a mess as Truman had become, he was very reverent about his art. That was not to be wasted, and these boxes, they were a work of art, almost religious. Find the story, tell it, but never make fun of it afterward. That was as sacred to him as any golden rule a southern lawyer had ever taught her.

She knocked the boxes over with a swipe of her forearm so she wouldn't have to look at them anymore.

So they wouldn't have to look at her, not getting it.

So she could quit thinking.

So the dead could have their dignity, their all-knowing eyes weighted down with pennies.

And there it was, what Truman had wanted her—and only her—to see, and understand, all along.

It was on the bottom of the boxes, as careful a part of the design as everything on top had been.

She hadn't even looked at the bottoms before, even though the slithering snake had been guiding her there the whole time.

On the bottom, another picture of a snake had been cut into three sections, each part pasted on a separate bottom. Individually, it looked abstract; you couldn't tell what it was. But put them together, unbroken, and there was no mistaking it: it was a snake.

And underneath the snake was a single word, made up of a letter on the bottom of each box.

On the bottom of the first box, an M, made up of two tall Marilyn Monroes on either side, a strand of pearls in a V shape linking them together.

M is for Marilyn.

On the second box, an A, two mirror images of Gregory Peck

as Atticus, leaning in on himself like a teepee, shaking hands with himself so that his outstretched hand became the bar across the two slants of the A.

A is for Atticus.

And on the third box, under the head of the snake, was an N: three pictures of Truman's favorite, Nancy Clutter, from a high school yearbook picture, where she was in a cheerleader uniform, leading the team on to victory. Long, vertical pictures that formed the three lines of the letter.

N is for Nancy.

On top, a snake.

On the bottom, the word man.

Snake Man.

The two figures of a boy and girl on top of the box, looking down into something—the Snake Man's grave.

It's something only Truman and Nelle would know about, unless he'd told over the years. She hadn't. They'd sworn to keep it a secret all those years ago, and she'd kept her word.

That was the story he was telling.

That's where she had to go now, deeper into the cemetery, to the Snake Man's grave.

—

Assassins were after Truman, trying to steal his book and all its secrets. If he could just get to the sacred spot in the desert where he'd found the dead snake, he'd be safe.

His book would be safe.

The spirit of Nancy would protect them both.

He'd finally figured it out, watching Johnny Carson. The

world thought Bernadette Peters was singing "Thank You for Being a Friend," but only Truman knew what she was really saying, when she looked directly at the camera and spoke to him, in a cleverly disguised melody: "The Assassins are coming. Get out now, friend."

The assassins had broken into the Clutter house, they'd cut their telephone wires, but he wouldn't let them break into his house. He didn't want them hurting Myrtle; this was his fault, not hers. He had to lead them into the desert, away from the house. If he could just get a call in to Liz Smith and tell her, then they'd disappear. Assassins couldn't handle bad publicity any more than he could; if she published their names, they'd leave him alone once and for all.

He had to get to a safe house with a phone to call her, somewhere through the desert.

He hadn't planned the trip well: he'd run out of the house without a jacket, or a map, or his lucky shorts.

Just the pages of his book the wind hadn't blown away.

He had to keep it safe.

It was all he had left.

They'd taken everything else, but they couldn't take this.

He shivered; the night sky was a dark, hot color, but it wasn't keeping him warm.

Heliotrope: it was the color of the dark flower his beautiful swan, Babe Paley, had loved so much; she was a thing of beauty, just like the flower, before she'd turned ugly on him.

Face it, before he'd turned ugly on her, on all of them, and spilled their secrets to the world in some short stories.

He shivered again and saw the cold truth for just a moment.

He deserved what he got.

He had no more to give.

All he wanted was to be remembered.

Cold truths, for so late at night.

He'd left some writing that would be remembered, but the book he'd been working on for years . . . in the years to come, nobody would even remember who his beautiful ladies, his swans, were, or that there was a time when they ruled the world.

The only thing people would remember is that he never finished it.

He never even wrote it, most of it.

That was the coldest truth of all.

He'd been planning a party for nothing.

Page after page of nothing, literally. After the stories that had been published in Esquire, there was nothing. Just blank pages, after the first few on which he'd written the word heliotrope over and over, trying to find his way into the story. But there was nothing else there; it was a Missouri bankroll, a few real pages on the outside, nothing but fakes in the middle.

It was a truth that was too hard to hold for long.

Truman shivered again, and the comforting fog of illusion settled back over him. It started in his toes and went all the way up to the crown of his head and out to his fingertips: a shiver, a release, an orgasm as his whole body shook and the rest of the pages of the book flew into the sky, released to the enveloping silence of the night.

Now, nobody would get it. Rather that, than it get into the assassins' hands. He'd been planning to send it to Nelle for safe-keeping—all his boxes and clues had been building up to that—but even that he couldn't be sure about. He hadn't left things good with her; she might not guard it like he wanted her to. Oh, well;

he was glad he had tried to make things right with her by sending her the other thing instead; it should be there by now.

He held his hands high for a moment of blessing, no longer holding onto anything.

He was free, rid of it all.

He fell to his knees, and that's when he saw it.

Another sign.

"And I shall send signs and wonders," the Good Book said.

He hadn't read a good book in ages.

It must have been trapped behind, when they flew their kites for Nancy. Now, it was so clear, so obvious, that it had been waiting for him, whipping in the breeze. He could send it off, to the place where it would do the most good; it would be the final part of the message he had been planning for so long, once he'd started his long good-bye.

Now, he just had to make his way through the desert, to the post office and a phone that worked, and hope the assassins didn't get him first.

—

Far behind, Myrtle and Danny saw the pages in the sky, dazzling white against dark blood red. They snatched them out of the air and followed them like a trail of bread crumbs.

—

Nelle made her way to the Snake Man's grave, her eyes growing narrow and silver like those of a wolf that could see and smell its prey in the dark.

But someone else had gotten there first.

Nelle had seen the figure before, but she couldn't remember where.

She got the gun ready.

She couldn't wait for memory to come.

The black-covered figure was so intent on its job—saying a silent prayer at the grave, holding out a brown-paper-covered box like an offering at Delphi—it didn't hear her approach. It didn't hear tennis shoes in the dewy grass or the rusty hammer of a pistol click into place.

But Nelle had to see who it was before she shot it, even if it was about to desecrate another grave by burying the parcel it held. It had struck once at her brother Ed's grave; she couldn't let it do its evil work again. Defending the grave, or attacking the creature, Nelle didn't know and didn't care; she just wanted the person gone.

She reached forward just as the creature bent down and stuck a small hand shovel in the ground, making the first cut in the Snake Man's grave.

Nelle grabbed, and the person whipped around in shock.

Nelle stared face to face at herself.

Or at least, a woman very much like herself.

Old before her time.

Lost.

Her hair gray, the kind of gray that only comes from grief you carry for decades.

Nelle was looking in the face of Sally Boular.

Son's sister.

Boo Radley's sister, whose scream that the Klan had grabbed her brother had put a stop to Truman's Halloween party all those years ago.

Now, two old women stared at each other, their weapons frozen in midair: a rusty garden trowel and a gun that probably wouldn't even fire anymore.

Nelle would have laughed, if it hadn't been the saddest thing she had ever seen. "Oh, my God! Sally. You."

Nelle couldn't laugh; she could barely breathe.

"Why?"

"Why not? Truman called to find out if I was still alive, to do his bidding. Barely, I said, after what *you* did to us . . . You made my brother a laughingstock! A bogeyman! You dug up his grave for all the world to see . . . now I'm digging up yours. Boo Radley . . ."

Sally spit it out, like acid in Nelle's face, acid Nelle had been bracing for for years. Boo Radley, Son Boular, Sally's brother, whom Nelle had turned into a character for the ages to fear, to pity, to know.

Sally hadn't wanted anybody to know him.

People poking, and prying, and trying to figure out the truth.

"What did he ever do to you? He was my brother. You had one too. Don't you remember? Don't you remember what it was like, hanging onto his every word, wanting him to love you, to be his best friend. And then, doing everything you could to protect him, to save him, to shield him, no matter what anybody said? What YOU said?"

Nelle didn't have an answer, on this sacred spot—except that she had been there, he was part of her childhood, too.

She thought she had honored him.

Just what Truman had done to Nancy Clutter.

"You, of all people," Sally continued. "With that sister of yours. You'd kill anyone who said anything against her, yet it was just fine for you to ruin my brother. Poor boy who never hurt a fly. Now I'M the one left to clean up all the mess."

"Sally, I made him famous."

"You made him a grotesque. Just like you've become. You deserve this heartache from Truman. Wish I'd thought of it first. He set it all in motion, with one phone call: follow her, take her picture, deliver the boxes he sent, come here, to your most secret place . . ."

Sally thrust the box she'd been about to bury at Nelle.

"But the funny thing is: Truman said he was doing it . . . to make up to you. He wouldn't tell me for what. I told him you could never make up for what you did to me . . . I've done my job now, it's yours. Let the dead bury the dead. I can stop."

Sally walked away, but she didn't seem any lighter, relieved of something. She looked even more weighted down, as if the pain would never leave.

Nelle's knees wouldn't hold up as she watched Sally Boular disappear. She buckled and fell, almost a dead weight, on top of the Snake Man's grave, like the handfuls of earth she and Truman had tossed on top of his coffin so many years ago.

She'd reached the end, whatever it was. Sally would never forgive her; that was clear. Had she done wrong, using Son's life? Had Truman done wrong, using the Clutters, and all his swans? Did all the people who came to Monroeville, wanting to know Nelle, wanting to know her and even own her after the story she'd shared with them—had they all done wrong?

They were all grave robbers, herself included, taking what didn't belong to them.

But were they grave givers, too—was there such a word? There was now, Nelle decided, in that very place; they gave back, made honor of lives that would have been forgotten.

They hadn't meant to hurt anybody.

They'd just become fascinated.

All she had to do now was open the package Sally had left with her, and her hurt would be over.

But she couldn't open it, not yet.

She didn't know if she wanted it to be over, or to keep going.

It had brought her back alive, this game Truman had played, and almost killed her at the same time.

For some reason, for all the reasons in the world, she couldn't stop crying, as she propped herself up on top of the Snake Man's grave.

—

Truman called it "doing a geographic": traveling someplace he wanted to go without ever leaving home. It might be somewhere new, or somewhere he'd spent years; it didn't matter. He'd pull together art books about the place (say, China or Paris), prepare an appropriate menu—fresh-brewed coffee and piping hot croissants and the best marmalade, put on an Edith Piaf record, and there he'd be.

Voilà.

Now, he could do it by merely closing his eyes; he didn't even need the props anymore.

Now, as he crossed the Palm Springs desert on this cold night, he did a geographic of his own death.

It was the only way to get warm.

Step by step, clutching the final sign he'd been given, he imagined his body in a coffin, on fire. That's how he wanted to go, by cremation, and he imagined the flames licking their way over his body and to the top of his head, setting free all the words and memories that were trapped there.

He thought it was a geographic of his death, but it was really a geographic of his life.

The flames started on his feet.

They were closest to earth, the coldest.

He was three, in a hotel room in New Orleans with the mother he barely knew. She'd taken him from his cousins and promised to be a good mother, but she was already being bad, the way she scolded him all the time. She was dressing to go out, powdering her body after stepping out of the bath. Her skin was silky and smooth, because she put bubbles of oil in the water. If he stayed in the water too long, his skin got all wrinkly, but hers got even smoother, and she made it smoother still by dusting powder all over it. He used her like a giant slide, careening down the hills of her silky smooth legs and suffocating himself in her, pressing his little-boy nose to her skin and inhaling, because he didn't know how much longer she would be his and he wanted to breathe in everything he could. When her skin wasn't enough, he drowned himself in the pink chiffon dress she had picked out for the night, rolling himself up in it like he'd roll in the bed-covers, and she got mad at him again. She said he had to stay behind and be a good boy while she went to see his daddy, but he knew it wasn't his daddy she was going to see in the hot New Orleans night. She sprayed a whiff of Evening in Paris perfume into the air and walked through it, like a model on a runway walking through a cloud, and he imitated her, running instead of walking through the mist, arms out like a plane, and they both laughed, even though she was mad at him, and he wanted to be just like her, beautiful in pearls and going out for the night, and she shimmered into the dress, put a magic spell on it so it flew into the air and stayed there until she said "Abracadabra," and only then did it fall gently onto her body. He positioned himself so that the soft folds of the skirt enveloped him as well, and it was his dress, too, they'd share it, but she was leaving him, his mommy was leaving him, and he didn't know where she was going, so he scooted his little legs to the door and ran smack into it as it closed in front of him, and he couldn't hide under her pretty pink skirt anymore, and all he could touch was wood, but it wasn't soft, and he heard a key turning in a lock and he knew that was the sound of him being left alone. It was the sound of his terror and his mother saying "I don't love you and I never did," and he made a sound of his own, which, because he knew no words, or knew them only in his head but couldn't make them come out right on his tongue and lips, was a scream, and he made it as loud and high as anything that had ever been heard in the history of the world, and suddenly there were bangs on the wall, and he thought there's Mother, she knows she did wrong, she knows she has to come back and get me, but she's lost her key, and she can't get back in. But it wasn't his mother, she was long gone to some stranger outside, and the night and the moon and the stars disappeared and there had never been a room as dark as this before, and he grabbed her bottle of Evening in Paris perfume and crawled under the bed with it, where it was even darker, but at least nothing could find him when he hid under the bed, and he drank and drank and drank from the bottle so he could have his mother inside him forever . . .

. . . and now the flames were at his groin . . .

. . . and that's when he saw Perry, hiding under the bed, too, watching his own mother who didn't even bother to go out for her men, but brought them back to the room, so drunk she didn't even mind that her little boy could watch, she barely even knew he was there, and Perry could look out from under the bed and see two pairs of feet on the floor, but his mother's shoes weren't pretty, they were all broken down, and the man wore boots that had mud all over them . . .

. . . and the flames were melting Truman's hips and licking at his stomach now . . .

. . . and he was under the bed with Perry, and they were looking at the feet together—Perry looking at the flat feet of his mother, and Truman looking at his mother's beautiful arched feet in sharp, pointy shoes—and Truman hugged Perry because he needed a man to take care of him and wrap his strong tattooed arms around him, that would keep him from being scared as long as he could wrap his arms around him . . .

. . . and it hurt for just a minute because the fire was at his heart . . .

. . . and now Nelle would take care of him, that's where she lived, in his heart, better than any man, and they went to a funeral together, the funeral of the Snake Man, and Nelle said she was afraid of being buried alive, and he told her they would drill a hole in the coffin and tie a string to her big toe, so that if she ever woke up inside and it was all dark, all she had to do was pull at the string and he would come running. It was special magic string and nothing could break it; he'd tie it to a bell in his room and it would ring any time of the day or night if it got pulled . . .

. . . and the fire was at his neck now, tickling his throat, and releasing all the sounds he'd held onto for so long . . .

. . . and now Truman was nearly sixty and he was the one in the coffin, but they'd forgotten to drill the hole or tie the string and he could feel the fire but he felt good, better than he had in years, because it was melting the fat off his body and he was getting lighter and freer and now he could fly, just like the butterflies he loved, the butterflies whose pictures he'd paste on kites, and he could see Sook holding the kite string on the other side, and he had to get to her so he started running faster to keep the kite aloft and keep ahead of the flames as they got to his brain, and he panicked because he thought they'd burn up all the words he had stored there, all the words for stories he had left to write, but as the fire released the words into the sky, he realized he had only a few words left, as he ran to Babe and Nina and Sook waiting for him on the other side . . .

Beautiful Babe . . .

Mama, it's me . . .

It's Buddy . . .

I'm cold . . .

Weeks later, they would be the last words he ever said, at Joanne Carson's house in Los Angeles, where he would crawl to die, like an animal who knew its time had come, but for now . . .

. . . Myrtle and Danny found him, inside the door of the post office, the part that was open all night long, huddled by the outgoing slot like he was waiting to be shipped out with the morning's post.

He'd found it, after all, Myrtle's secret sanctuary.

As she held him and rocked him and called him Precious Baby and wrapped him in Sook's scrap quilt, she knew he would go before her.

Her prayer had been answered.

She knew he wouldn't be alone, as he kept whispering those names, Babe and Mama and Sook . . .

He wouldn't be alone, with those people to guide the way.

Myrtle hoped she wouldn't be, when her time came. She even wondered—and hoped—Truman would come back for her.

She and Danny wrapped him up, and took him home, to wait.

—

Nelle had a match ready, a whole box of them, to burn whatever was inside the Snake Man's last box.

She still hadn't opened it.

Maybe she wouldn't; the others had all been Pandora's boxes, releasing evil into the world. She'd looked in the bottom of them all, after she'd emptied them out, and hadn't found any hope.

Why should this one be any different?

But it was different; she could feel it, literally. It was a different size than the others, much larger and heavier. Its heft, the exact way it sat in her hands, reminded her of something from her past, but she couldn't place it, not yet.

Sitting on the Snake Man's grave and leaning against his marker, she took a deep breath and unwrapped the paper; there was no collaged snakebite kit inside, no hand-carved coffin underneath that, no picture inside that—except for the one that formed in her brain when she finally realized what Truman had sent to her, by way of Boo Radley's sister.

The Book.

Her book.

He'd given her back her book, the copy of the manuscript she had given him to read on their way to Kansas the first time. On the cover page was the love letter he'd written to her, on that trip: "It's the book I wish I could have written. Truman."

All these years, she'd forgotten he had it, left in his room when she fled one night in the snow.

It was the proof she'd waited for her entire life—or that Alice had waited for—evidence, once and for all, that Nelle wrote The Book she'd always said she'd written, that Truman had nothing to do with it, no matter what he said.

All she had to do now was show them, show the world, show anyone who came to town to ask, and shove it in the faces of those who didn't dare. The manuscript was dated; scholars could compare it line by line to the published version and see that nothing had changed. They could analyze Truman's handwriting to prove it really was him who'd written on the cover page.

But she wouldn't.

What good would come of it?

People would still wonder, still accuse of her of some kind of fakery.

She didn't need to do it, to know what she'd written.

The doubt had almost made her forget what she'd known since all those years ago, when she and Truman sat together for three days on a train ride to Kansas.

It was freezing, and her life was about to begin.

—

Why they took a train instead of a plane she didn't know, except that Truman had become convinced they had to see the country from down low, they had to experience the transition from the mountains of the East to the flatness and nothingness of Kansas. He wanted to see the very first stalk of corn that came into view, the very first grain silo.

Nelle said you could see the same thing from a plane, even better.

"But can you reach out and touch it?" he said.

They took the train, and he put his hand out the window.

Three days for her to agonize, while he read her book, and the landscape turned from green and blue to yellow and finally dusty brown.

Finally, she couldn't wait any longer: she had to know what he thought.

He closed his eyes, choosing his words as carefully as an epigraph he would commit to print: "You've done something better than even I could do: you've written the perfect book about childhood, from your heart. I used to know how, but I've forgotten. Somehow, I think going to Kansas will show me the way, again . . . the way back to what you've already found."

He kissed her cheek and fell asleep with his head on her shoulder, like they used to do when they were little. She turned and looked out the window onto a changing landscape, racing past with blurry scenes from her life.

She was six, hiding in a chinaberry tree with her best friend.

Seven, he dragged her along to see a stranger get buried.

Nine, she stood on tiptoes and looked in a knothole on the tree, to see if he'd sent her a present from his new home in New York.

Eleven, she cried, she missed him so much.

Thirteen, she grew up and was forced to wear a dress for the first time.

Eighteen, she left Eden, and went off to school.

Twenty-three, she moved to a different Eden searching for her old friend.

Twenty-five, she said good-bye to her mother and brother, forever.

Twenty-seven, she started remembering what it was like to be a child, and began writing it all down.

Thirty, she had written her first book.

Thirty, she was on her way to a grand adventure, with her strange best friend from childhood.

Thirty, she shivered in the cold and delight of the night, everyone asleep in the dark railroad car except for her, and said a prayer of thanks for being alive.

Thirty, on a night train speeding into Kansas, and she wanted to remember the moment forever. She blew on the window and made a cloud to write her name on, to prove she'd been there.

—

Now, in her fifties, propped up against the Snake Man's tombstone, granite for a pillow instead of feathers, Nelle was dreaming, instead of remembering:

Truman shifted in the seat next to her, but when she looked at him, he had aged. The hollows under his eyes were deep, and his skin was marked with little explosions of blood vessels. No amount of plastic surgery, of skin pulled tight everywhere, could disguise the fact that she was looking at a death mask.

He got up out of his seat on the railroad car and reached in the berth overhead for his suitcase.

Something was wrong. Truman would never reach for his own suitcase; he'd have a porter do it. He was too short to reach the overhead bin, but his arms magically extended, just as hers had when she reached into their tree just days ago, in a dream.

"I'm tired, Nelle. I'm leaving."

"But we aren't there yet."

"I've been everywhere I've ever wanted to go. I don't need to go anywhere else."

"I kept waiting for you to call back . . ."

"I ran out of words, used 'em all up. I couldn't think of anything else to say. I thought the boxes could take over, speak for me, give you a new story to write . . . You were such a good writer."

"That's a lot of history to put on some boxes. Cardboard and paste and pictures."

"I know."

He really had run out of words, this great poet who was now as silent, as sheepish, as Kenyon Clutter had been.

"I've done my job now, it's yours. Let the dead bury the dead. I can stop."

The very same words Sally Boular had said to her.

"I stopped a long time ago, except for hurting people."

"But why?"

A question, like the ones she had asked Bonnie Clutter and Kenyon, that didn't have an answer.

Nelle looked out the train window one last time: she was old, and the tired man who'd been sitting next to her, keeping her warm, walked off with a suitcase and a book in his hand, and left her behind.

The year was 1984.

Nelle awoke with a start, leaning against the Snake Man's mossy grave, and knew that Truman was dying.

She was surprised she felt as sad as she did.

She looked around the cemetery as if she might catch him walking there, among the paths to Eden, as he had once called them. But there was no Truman, no ghost, although there would be one, soon enough.

In seconds, it was as if she'd finally learned we don't get ghosts of those we love the most, we just get dreams of them, and memories. Memories of loves that had come and gone; some Truman had foreseen, some he hadn't. Ghosts were left to relative strangers, like Bonnie and Kenyon. Real ghosts, of real people we loved, would scare us too much, remind us too much.

Most times, a dream was as much of a good-bye as we'd ever get.

But now, Nelle got something else, too; a return to something, and a lightning's flash of understanding: why Truman had said what he had at the Clutters' grave, why he had fought with Nelle there, about ending the book with Alvin Dewey and Nancy's best friend Susan meeting there, when they hadn't in real life.

Real life wasn't all it was cracked up to be, he'd said then, and Nelle, of all people, had gotten mad.

Some lies were good, if they kept people from hurting.

Some lies were good, if they brought peace.

That's what Truman had been trying to say back then, but Nelle hadn't wanted to listen. Maybe that was his good-bye to her, so long ago.

The morning sun was coming up; it was time to go. Alice would be worried. Enough of visiting graves. She'd be back, soon enough, for good. She patted the earth back into place, and began to make her way home. She even laughed a little; she didn't know why, but it felt good for a change.

For now, she was alive.

It was time to go home.

—

A few days later, another package will arrive at Nelle's house, an address hastily scribbled on it. But somehow, this one won't scare her as she tears it open. Inside, there will be no box, no coffin, no picture, just a jumble of sticks and white paper and cut-out letters and string. Nelle will see, with the eyes of the child she once was, that it had been a kite. She will take her time to smoothe out its wrinkles and mend its breaks, take it outside and run to get it up in the air. There, she will finally see the words that Truman had once sailed up to Nancy Clutter, that had been lost for a time in a Palm Springs desert. Now, they will seem to unfurl only for her: "I'm Sorry," the message on the kite will read, as it takes flight into the clouds.

Author's Note

I knew of Harper Lee long before I knew of Truman Capote—sort of. My older brother Porky took my twin brother Tim and me to see the movie of *To Kill a Mockingbird* when we were just six or seven; he must have thought we were too young to understand and thus be disturbed by the rape of Miss Mayella Ewell. He was right—that part went right over my head, although I knew it was something "bad"—but far more disturbing, in a way Porky couldn't have foreseen, was one of the final scenes of the movie. Late at night, in those haunting black and white shadows, Jem and Scout are walking home after their school agricultural pageant and get attacked by a drunken Bob Ewell, Mayella's father. Scout, encased in her "ham" costume, is knocked to the ground, and witnesses the rest of the attack through a prism of chicken wire, papier mache, and terror. She awakens back at home, to find that Boo Radley has been her savior, and that her father would watch after her broken-armed brother, in what for me became the most glorious sentence to ever end a book: "He would be there all night, and he would be there when Jem waked up in the morning." After a childhood of broken arms, an absent father, and terrors both imagined and real and only partially glimpsed, I wanted, somehow, to live inside that story.

Somewhere down the road, I discovered that Harper Lee had based the character of Dill Harris—all buck teeth and fancy outfits and indignation, just like me—on her childhood buddy, Truman Capote. I didn't quite know who he was, but I knew he was important, and I pretended to understand why.

Then I saw the movie of *In Cold Blood*. (A fact of my small-town Texas growing-up: I saw the movies of most books before I read them.) Now a new and different scene came to haunt my childhood: the scene of Nancy Clutter being shot to death in her farmhouse bedroom, after so softly pleading, "Please. Don't." Years later in New York, I met the actress who played Nancy, and all I could do was babble incoherently, and ask how she survived filming that scene, what scar it must have left on her; what scar it left on me, just watching it. When I found out that Harper had been Truman's assistant—that the two writers who had most haunted my childhood had been together, in that haunted place in Kansas—I couldn't get over it. I thought I alone knew the secret of what must be the greatest story never told.

Those were the underpinnings, so long ago, of *Capote in Kansas*— their fractured childhood next door to each other in Monroeville, Alabama; their reunion, over two decades later, in Kansas. Parts of those events have been well-documented, in many books and articles; the rest of the novel is a product of my life-long fascination, imagination, and even obsession. During the writing and research of this book, I consulted many sources; the two primary ones were Gerald Clarke's masterful biography *Capote* and George Plimpton's oral biography *Truman Capote*. Any factual errors, whether deliberate or unintentional, are entirely my own.

A surprising amount of the book is based on real events, beginning with the childhood Halloween party that Truman threw, and Son and Sally Boular's attempt to join it, only to be rescued from the Klan by Nelle's father Amasa. (Son did in fact die of pneumonia when he was thirty, after having spent the bulk of his life in his father's house, but Sally's reaction to Nelle is entirely a product of my own imagination.)

In broad outline, my account of the writing of *In Cold Blood* and *To Kill a Mockingbird* are based on fact, as are the existence of Harper's sister Alice and the deaths of Harper's mother and older brother Ed, within five weeks of each other. However, their private thoughts about each other, the details of their burials, the letters that Harper writes to her dead brother, and most certainly her travels to a nearby cemetery (that may or may not exist) are my own invention. Perhaps most audaciously, I have placed her at two events where I know she wasn't present: Truman's legendary Black and White Ball at the Plaza (she was, of course, invited); and his night of "bar-hopping" in Kansas City. Truman did, almost unbelievably for that time and place, take Detective Nye and his wife as well as another couple from a drag show to a gay bar to a lesbian bar. Harper was not there, and any of the attitudes or feelings my "character" Harper Lee expresses during that night are my own.

Myrtle Bennett, Truman's housekeeper during his time in Palm Springs, was a real person; at one point a Cotton Club dancer as I have written, Truman did in fact promise he would stake her in her own maid service. I'm sure the real Myrtle was much more aware of Truman's fame and writings than I have made her, but one unfortunate fact I did not invent was her death from cancer. In reality, she died before Truman, and he was reportedly devastated by it. Of all the characters in the book, she is the one I would most like to have met. "Danny," as Truman called him, was also a real lover of Truman's during that period, but several of the events in which he participates (the stealing of the book manuscript, the "sugar-bombing" of his gas tank) are composites of others in Truman's life.

One of the most tantalizing—and to me, little-known details I discovered about Truman—were his "snake boxes," as I call them. He began constructing these mysterious and evocative artworks late in his life, and they were exhibited at Manhattan's Gotham Book Mart after his death. (When Truman approached Gotham's Andreas Brown about his long-in-the-works "secret project," Brown at first thought it might be Truman's finished manuscript for *Answered Prayers*.) Many of the boxes were sold; some were left to friends in Truman's will. More recently, a number of them were sold at auction. I was fascinated by them, but the use to which I put them is entirely my own.